The Case of the Grandfather Clock

*Also by Roberta Updegraff
in Large Print:*

The Baffling Bequest
Puzzle in Patchwork

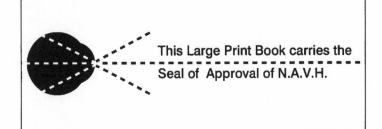

GUIDEPOSTS

CHURCH CHOIR MYSTERIES™

The Case of the Grandfather Clock

CANCEL

Roberta Updegraff

Thorndike Press • Waterville, Maine

Copyright © 2002 by Guideposts, Carmel, New York 10512.

Published in 2005 by arrangement with
Guideposts Book Division.

Thorndike Press® Large Print Christian Mystery.

The tree indicium is a trademark of Thorndike Press.

The text of this Large Print edition is unabridged.
Other aspects of the book may vary from the original edition.

Set in 16 pt. Plantin by Liana M. Walker.

Printed in the United States on permanent paper.

Library of Congress Cataloging-in-Publication Data

Updegraff, Roberta.
    The case of the grandfather clock / by Roberta Updegraff.
        p. cm. — (Church choir mysteries) (Thorndike Press
        large print Christian mysteries)
        ISBN 0-7862-8007-7 (lg. print : hc : alk. paper)
        1. Church musicians — Fiction. 2. Choirs (Music) —
    Fiction. 3. Cats — Fiction. 4. Large type books. I. Title.
    II. Series. III. Thorndike Press large print Christian
    mystery series.
    PS3621.P38C37 2005
    813'.6—dc22   2005016348

To my brother and friend,
Daniel Carson Blair.
Thanks for always being there for me.
You've been the best of supporters.

As the Founder/CEO of NAVH, the only national health agency solely devoted to those who, although not totally blind, have an eye disease which could lead to serious visual impairment, I am pleased to recognize Thorndike Press* as one of the leading publishers in the large print field.

Founded in 1954 in San Francisco to prepare large print textbooks for partially seeing children, NAVH became the pioneer and standard setting agency in the preparation of large type.

Today, those publishers who meet our standards carry the prestigious "Seal of Approval" indicating high quality large print. We are delighted that Thorndike Press is one of the publishers whose titles meet these standards. We are also pleased to recognize the significant contribution Thorndike Press is making in this important and growing field.

Lorraine H. Marchi, L.H.D.
Founder/CEO
NAVH

* Thorndike Press encompasses the following imprints: Thorndike, Wheeler, Walker and Large Print Press.

Acknowledgments

Thanks, all the wonderful support folks in my life. Hugs to my darling husband Mark for running umpteen errands, taking over the taxi service and, most of all, giving me lots of encouragement (the massages were great, too). Kisses to Katie (our youngest and only child still at home) for being a good sport about being forgotten or picked up late. *Abbracci* to our exchange student Dario Recalcati for all the pick-me-ups, cups of coffee and Italian cookies that appeared at my computer just when I needed a break.

Special thanks to Eileen M. Berger, my wonderful mentor and friend, for brainstorming the plot with me. I appreciate all the support you've given me through the years. Hugs to Roberta Brosious for all your help — you are the dearest of friends. Kudos to all the West Branch Christian Writers and St. David's Christian Writer's Association. I appreciate you all!

Accolades to my great editors at Guideposts Books and Inspirational Media Division! Michele Slung does a great job of making my manuscript read better, and Stephanie Castillo Samoy is even sweeter in person. Thanks, ladies, for the wonderful day in New York City. I appreciate you all more than words can convey!

1

"He's okay." Dr. Wright slipped his arm around Gracie Parks's shoulders and ushered her into the front room of Hammie Miller's little cabin on Acorn Lake. "I didn't want to worry you — I just needed to know what medication he was on. He seems fine now, but I'll continue to monitor him."

Gracie sent a prayer heavenward, thankful that Bill Wright had been with Uncle Miltie. She'd not really worried when he told her he was going on a fishing trip with the owner of Miller's Feed Store and some other pals. Despite his osteoarthritis, he was as game as he was good-humored — but, still, he was by far the oldest in the group.

Heat exhaustion, it turned out, was the culprit.

"I probably shouldn't have called you, but I needed to be sure exactly what doses he was taking," the doctor was saying. "Of course, Gracie, you realize it wouldn't have hurt to stay put until I called you back! It could have saved you a trip out here." He looked at her with affectionate reproach.

Gracie felt a twinge of embarrassment for panicking and racing out to the cabin. Hammie's weekend place was over an hour from Willow Bend. "I guess I was being a little over-protective," she admitted.

He laughed. "He's lucky to have you."

"We're lucky to have each other." She looked over to where her uncle was stretched out in a mammoth red recliner, with a compress made from a hand towel on his forehead. Their close friend Rocky Gravino sat in a chair beside him.

Rocky, owner and editor of the local paper, the *Mason County Gazette*, was only an honorary regular at the feed store. A late-in-life arrival in Willow Bend, Indiana, he'd lost his own wife years earlier. So, when Gracie's adored husband Elmo had died, it seemed only natural that Rocky would take a special interest in her well-being. After all, he and El had grown to be the best of friends.

He stood to offer her his chair. "The old goat gave us a scare." He chuckled, but Gracie could see the relief in Rocky's eyes.

"I'm really sorry, Gracie. I should have looked out for him better. But when I say *goat,* you know I mean he has the tenacity of one!"

Uncle Miltie overheard him and said gruffly, "It was my own stupid fault. Don't blame anyone else."

"It's been an unseasonable scorcher of a weekend, as you know," Bill Wright told her. "But it was my job to see that he stayed hydrated."

"I stayed in all day yesterday myself, or most of it," Gracie admitted. "And the choir loft was pretty steamy this morning." She gently stroked her uncle's cheek. He was still a bit flushed. "You're sure he's all right, Bill?"

"Of course, I'm all right!" Uncle Miltie pushed the lever to straighten the recliner. "Fit as a fiddle and ready to show up these young fellas, any day!"

Lester Twomley looked to Gracie. "He says that now, but you should have seen him an hour or so ago. One minute he's telling a joke as corny as the entire state of Kansas, the next he's staring blankly into space. Sure scared me!"

"Scared us all," Rocky agreed. "Never saw anything like it."

"I was right behind him," Bill explained to

Gracie. "I grabbed his elbow, so he wouldn't fall."

"Huh!" Uncle Miltie said. "It was like in one of those silent movies I grew up with. He swept me off my feet quicker than a Saturday serial hero catching a swooning damsel."

"It might have been funny, if it hadn't been so serious," Bill Wright reminded him.

Rocky looked at him. "It could have happened to any of us, I guess."

"That's right."

Uncle Miltie, hearing this, suddenly brightened. He gave Gracie a fast glance that hovered on the brink of an I-told-you-so.

Bill Wright went on. "The sun combines with the reflection off the water, and all of a sudden, *wham,* you don't know what hit you."

"Naw, I knew better," Uncle Miltie unexpectedly admitted. "I was feeling the heat after lunch, but I chose to ignore the warning signs. But we had us a wager, now, didn't we? I couldn't renege on my partners."

Gracie shot a suspicious look at each of the six men in turn. "Wager? What wager? You all were fishing, weren't you? Even when he plays pinochle, Uncle Miltie manages to stay upright."

She fixed her gaze on the newspaper editor. Rocky flashed her a sheepish grin.

"Blame me, Gracie. I egged Rocky on." Rocky's old pal Grover Wills now spoke up. "Nobody was catching anything but an earful of his boasting, so I suggested a little wager."

"Rocky did snag something," Uncle Miltie corrected, chuckling. "It prompted quite a discussion."

"It put up a fight!" Rocky defended.

Uncle Miltie laughed.

"It *could* have been Old Hammerhead," Lester offered.

"Hammerhead? That old legend's for real?" Gracie's eyes sparkled.

"The fish that won't be caught!" Hammie confirmed. "Nobody's ever seen him, mind you, but we're all sure he exists. They say he's as big as a shark and twice as ugly."

Grover shot Gracie a sly smile. "But there are a lot of tree roots in that part of the cove, if you get my drift."

"It put up a fight!" Rocky crossed his arms.

"Or, you snagged something with a little snap to it. Fish-like, let us say." Lester grinned at Grover. "Human imagination is a powerful force."

Gracie was starting to enjoy this. If Uncle Miltie was out of danger, then it was fun to see Rocky get some of what he was so willing to dish out.

"I'm telling you, that was a fish! Not a root, not a rock, not a shoe, not a branch! I pulled, and it pulled back. Find me a root that starts swimming away!" Rocky was scowling.

"That's how this all got started," Hammie explained. "We were giving Rocky grief about the one that got away, and then Grover launched into a story about a big one of his own."

Rocky rolled his eyes. "What you might call a whopper of a tale."

"Anyway," Hammie went on, "the next thing you knew, they started arguing about who was the better fisherman."

"Fish or cut bait, that's what I told him!" Grover declared. "Were we going to redeem our poor showing or not?"

"You mean, the fish's poor showing!" Uncle Miltie quipped.

"Remember that week on the Upper Peninsula?" Grover now asked. "Who caught *that* big one, my good fellow?"

"Luck!" Rocky scowled again.

Gracie now said, "You and Rocky have had some pretty great times, haven't you?"

"Yeah, we go way back. We've been competing since college, with Gravino usually beating me out in the brains department."

"So, you were . . . what?" Rocky regarded his friend's paunch. "Surely not the brawn?"

"Look who's talking!" The two men liked to tease each other about who had gained the most weight over the years.

Then Grover grew pensive. He walked to the bay window overlooking the water. "It's been too many years since I've been here at the lake. But it's good to come back — and under happier circumstances.

"My brother used to own the next place down. For me, fishing's always been just a great pastime, but to Franklin it was more than that. The sky, the forest beyond, even the ripples on the water — I guess you could say he found fishing a spiritual experience."

Gracie knew this was a moment to send up a quick prayer for Grover. Instinctively she understood that there was some pocket of deep pain hidden behind his memories of his brother.

"Franklin was a good man," Hammie said. "I hadn't realized until you told me that he'd died."

"Yeah, I know. He always regretted not keeping in touch. But you can understand.

It was just too hard."

Gracie looked hard at Rocky, knowing he'd understand that. Later, she'd want an explanation of what had happened to Franklin Wills. Grover, whom she'd met before, she knew was an FBI agent in Chicago.

"Getting back to our little wager, I was looking out for your interests, Gracie," Uncle Miltie said, changing the subject. "Well, the choir's interests, that is. But then, they're usually one and the same."

Gracie looked at him and smiled. His heart was as big as the entire state of Indiana, she thought sometimes.

"I said we should make the winner of the pot, the one of us with the biggest fish at the end of the weekend, fork over a contribution for those bells you guys have been wanting."

The choir of the Eternal Hope Community Church had been hoping for a set of bells ever since they'd attended a sacred music festival in Chicago, where they'd rejoiced to hear a renowned bell choir give a concert. It had been not just an inspiration to them, but a challenge.

Rocky now said, "Then again, with our luck running the way it is, maybe we should just try for a fish fry, instead, and rely on the Willow Mart's frozen fillets!"

Grover, who looked grateful that Uncle

Miltie had inadvertently steered the conversation away from his brother, now reminded them, "Rocky's right. We'd probably have been better off stocking the lake with fish fingers!"

"There's nothing you can do if your worm ain't trying," Uncle Miltie told them. He brightened. "Hey, that reminds me of a joke!"

Hammie groaned. "Cancel the ambulance! He's recovered!"

Gracie glanced around the room at the assembled men, each of whom clearly adored her uncle. They were all connected in different ways, and the feed store was only part of the equation.

Grover and Rocky were old friends, the newspaperman relying on the FBI agent for unofficial help from time to time. Bill Wright, she knew, played on a community softball team with Hammie, and was in the same league as Lester. El had played on the team with Bill, as well. She gave an inadvertent sigh, knowing how much her husband would have enjoyed this weekend getaway. How long had it been since she'd packed a cooler lunch for her own beloved eager angler? *And, dear Lord, You know there isn't a day that goes by that I don't miss him.*

"Anyone who's heard this joke before, you

can just be polite for a change. Remember, I'm an invalid!"

Uncle Miltie came by his nickname honestly. Like the late comedian, Milton Berle, who'd long ago kept America laughing with his droll television antics, Gracie's uncle, born George Morgan, had never met a punchline too corny to repeat.

"A little kid says to the Sunday school teacher," he now began. " 'Do you think Noah did a lot of fishing when he was on the ark?' 'I imagine he did,' says the teacher. The kid looks confused, and asks, 'With only two worms?' "

Uncle Miltie chuckled. "Just tell me if you didn't get it. Okay?"

"If you think we're not laughing because we didn't get it, then you've got another think coming," Rocky pronounced.

"Actually," said Gracie. "If I had that little boy in my Sunday school class, I'd probably be pleased he'd been putting two and two together — so to speak — so intelligently."

"Seriously now," Uncle Miltie said to them. "Did it ever occur to you that the early fish gets hooked by the same thing the early bird gets credit for? Where's the justice in that, I ask you?"

"About like finding ourselves on a fishing weekend with more bad jokes than bites! I don't know if we should thank the good doctor here for reviving you so brilliantly or heave him into the lake!" Rocky said, with mock menace.

At that moment the cabin's front door opened. Hammie looked up at the man entering the cabin. "Hey there! You remember Gracie Parks, Arlen's mom?"

Gracie now shook hands with Orville Miller, whom she knew had been only a few years ahead of her son Arlen in school. Quickly, however, Orville turned his attention to his older brother. "Didn't have any luck in the shed — there were just old books in those boxes!"

As Hammie suggested to him a couple of other places to look, Gracie observed the differences between them. Sartorially, at least, there was little resemblance, although physically the family relationship was obvious. When they spoke, their eyes crinkled similarly.

Hammie had on a well-worn flannel shirt with the tails hanging out of his jeans. His taller, slimmer brother was wearing brand-name outdoor clothing, all of it looking as if the price tags had been recently removed. Both men were blond and rosy cheeked.

Hammie explained to his guests that Orville was in search of their grandfather's old journals, for reasons that could possibly prove to be financially beneficial to them both.

"The truth is, I'm glad to have him home, no matter what the reason," Hammie told them, beaming.

Gracie was pretty sure, actually, that the brothers had had a falling-out, so it was heartening to see that any disagreements lingering between them had been set right again. She knew, too, that Hammie had inherited the family feed store and not Orville. *Thank You, Lord, for healing family ties that have been weakened.*

"One thing for sure," Orville now said, "in ten years, nothing's changed here at all."

Hammie corrected him. "That's not entirely true. But, then, I've never wanted to live any place else, and you wanted to make a life of your own. I understand that. Willow Bend, though, I promise you, isn't the same place you left a decade ago."

Orville explained, "I'm thinking of raising a few head of cattle, maybe do some experimental farming. I've got some investment property in central Pennsylvania."

Hammie looked at his brother with an expression Gracie couldn't read. "He happened to pick up some information on hybrid seed crops at the Pennsylvania State

Fair, and that reminded him of Grandpa's interest in the subject."

Orville didn't offer any further details. Still Gracie could tell he resented even the too-brief description of his intentions just given by Hammie. Whatever questions she might ordinarily have asked to be polite, she now decided the best thing was to be welcoming, no matter what. "It's nice to have you back, Orville. How long are you staying?"

"I'm not really sure," he replied. Then he added, offering a thin smile, "Of course, I should say, it all depends."

"Our grandfather developed a special strain of alfalfa seed," Hammie interjected. "It's still popular today — it's my best seller, in fact."

Orville nodded, but his smile stretched even thinner now. "Its success is what's inspired me. I think it's possible to improve on it."

Hammie looked at his brother proudly. Gracie hoped that he wouldn't be disappointed. She sternly admonished herself, *How can I pass judgment on anyone after an acquaintance — even if renewed — of only a few minutes? Dear Lord, I know it's not my place to judge at all.*

"We remember Grandpa keeping notebooks, so now we just have to turn them up. The good thing is that his office upstairs at the store is just like he left it. Dad never had the heart to get rid of anything, and I didn't either."

"A bunch of pack rats — the three of you!" Orville looked scornful. "But I guess I should be grateful, now that I need to track something down."

"Folks around here like the store the way it is. I know that," Hammie said mildly. "It's never hurt business."

"That's for sure," Uncle Miltie now put his two cents in. "Your place is part of the heart and soul of Willow Bend."

"It'll be front-page news when it changes, I can tell you that," Rocky offered. "But, in the meantime, I won't be writing any editorials demanding that Hammie modernize."

Gracie saw Orville's lip curl slightly, but he said nothing. Instead, he glanced around and her gaze followed his. What she observed was a well-lived-in room, offering just the right sort of shabby comfort for a lakeside cottage. The chairs were saggy, the hooked rugs faded, and vintage vacation memorabilia dotted every surface — that is, where books and papers and old magazines weren't piled and spilling over.

The gauze curtains gave a bounce in the

breeze. A splash of sunlight suddenly illuminated a dark corner of the room. Gracie now saw that a grandfather clock stood there, its hands frozen at half past six.

She wondered if the old clock had just run down, or if something had shocked the solitary sentry into silence.

2

Rocky insisted that Gracie stay the night. Even if Uncle Miltie was fine now, she'd had a scare. It was a wonder she'd managed to get there in one piece, worried as she'd been. He went on and on, citing traffic statistics.

She suspected, however, that he was really looking out for his stomach. With a great sigh of contented anticipation, he volunteered to fetch the ingredients for her shepherd's pie at the Acorn Lake convenience store. List in hand, he headed out with Grover, while Uncle Miltie excused himself for a nap.

The hot afternoon sun streamed across the water and through the cabin's windows. Once again it brought the grandfather clock out of the shadows, compelling Gracie to cross the room and admire it.

"Grandpa bought that for Grandma," Hammie told her. "She'd always wanted one, so he gave it to her the day my father was born."

"What a lovely gesture," Gracie said.

He went on to explain that his grandparents had built the cabin as their first home. Then, when Sam Miller had begun his feed business, they'd moved into Willow Bend.

"My grandfather was a diehard fisherman. He looked forward to retiring here one day. After Grandma died, though, the move didn't seem to make any sense. But this was where his heart was. Lots of happy memories here."

Gracie remembered how close he had been to his grandfather. Sam Miller had suffered from progressive dementia, and Hammie had taken care of him until almost the very end. He practically didn't even date until after the old man died. But, just when folks had decided that Hammie would probably remain a bachelor for the rest of his life, he'd met Sherry, the woman who became his wife.

"My grandparents spent every spare minute here when my dad was growing up. In some ways, the house in Willow Bend was less our home than this was. So here the old grandfather clock stayed, keeping perfect time, until my dad died."

Gracie looked at him. "It stopped the day your father died?"

She knew that Todd Miller had drowned on the lake years earlier. "Grandpa imagined the clock had stopped at the exact time of our father's death. At least, it suddenly wasn't working anymore and he drew his own conclusions."

"Pretty unlikely, if you ask me — Willow Bend's not the Bermuda Triangle!" Orville looked exasperatedly at his brother.

"Well, of course we don't know the exact time he died, but when the clock stopped, Grandpa decided to leave it that way. After he passed on, the business took most of my time and, for one reason or another, I just never have gotten up here much. I guess the truth is, I've never had the heart to restart it."

"We were kids when Dad died," Orville told Gracie. "Our mother was killed in a car accident shortly after that. I don't remember much about my parents. Grandpa raised us."

Memories were among Gracie's treasures. She couldn't imagine not having them to ease the grief. Blessedly, Arlen, her only child, had been grown and married when El died in an accident. Gracie imagined that for the Miller boys, the lack of memories of their parents had only added to the tragedy of their young lives.

Orville mused aloud, "So Grandpa wanted it kept that way? Maybe he even stopped it himself."

"Does it really matter?" Hammie asked his brother. "We just know it made him feel better, somehow, to believe that that clock shared his pain."

Hammie turned to Gracie. "He'd lost his only child, and then the daughter-in-law he loved."

The brothers exchanged glances, but Gracie felt unsure of their meaning. She knew Hammie well, but it was pretty clear Orville didn't entirely share his brother's deep affection for the grandfather who had raised them.

"We always had to do things his way," Orville said unexpectedly. "We didn't dare talk about the accidents, or anything surrounding them — ever. . . ."

"We have lots of other memories, though, good ones," Hammie said, breaking in. "Grandpa loved this place, in spite of what happened. I think the clock's silence was somehow comforting to him."

"You hang on to the past like you can bring it back!" Orville chided him. "But you can't!"

27

Hammie motioned Gracie toward the shelves full of books and bric-a-brac. "You can see how much the past meant to him just by looking around here. There's a story behind every little thing, and I loved those stories. The accidents were really the only thing he wouldn't talk about. We had a happy childhood here."

"For *you*, Hammie, that's true," Orville said. "To me, this place is a mausoleum. It's always given me the creeps. And I think he owed it to us to let us talk about our father's death."

"It was just his way," Hammie countered. "You know he hated arguing or even raising his voice. So, if something was bothering him, he kept it to himself."

"That doesn't make it right!" Orville shot back. "You've sanctified him, the way you've sanctified this place, and that store! He was an opinionated old coot who insisted on having everything his own way!"

Orville shot a glance toward the silent sentry. "Even that clock probably didn't dare cross him! It understood what you don't seem to, that he had a will of iron! You may have felt close to him, but I felt like a prisoner!" Hammie shook his head sorrowfully, but Orville simply clamped his lips firmly together.

Gracie looked at them and sighed to herself. Families were complicated, she understood, but love was stronger and more powerful than any conflict. She prayed for God to send these brothers the greater mutual understanding they needed.

After supper, Lester, Bill and Grover gathered around the table to watch the checkers game that Rocky and Uncle Miltie were finishing. Gracie scanned the bookshelves for reading material, finally selecting a book on Indiana marshlands.

Hammie handed her a cup of coffee. "Grandpa was also an avid conservationist. He was thrilled when Dad chose environmental studies as a major in college. And proud that Dad was an inventor of sorts, always tinkering with things.

"Dad helped in the store, all through high school. But he really didn't like all the details of managing a business, so he became a traveling salesman — for lawn tractors and other equipment."

She was curious. "But later you chose the store — working with your grandfather?"

"It just wasn't my dad's thing, but that doesn't mean it wasn't mine." Hammie picked up a framed photograph of his father pushing his mother on a swing. "Dad was a dreamer, our Aunt Polly always said. He enjoyed the traveling and preferred the flexible work schedule. Grandpa would finish his coffee by five in the morning and stay open as long as one customer was waiting. He worked long days, but that's what the clientele — almost all farmers in those days — demanded. But once he proved they could trust him, they were loyal to Miller's Feed with nary a complaint."

Hammie now grinned at Gracie. "I confess I used to get a little jealous because Orville seemed to be having all the fun. But I loved my grandfather and loved spending time with him. I never meant for him to single me out, to leave me the business after he died."

"You have nothing to apologize for, Hammie." Gracie touched his arm. "Your grandfather was a fair man. You were the child with the heart for his legacy. I remember how proud he was of you."

Hammie shrugged. "The funny thing is, he never said. And I think that's what got to Orville. Grandpa expected so much from us. He just took it for granted that we'd both come to work for him. The trouble was, Orville wanted his own life, just like our father."

Gracie remembered well the angular old

man in overalls joking with his customers, and how she had seen his mind deteriorate those last years of his life. He had died in a nursing home, unable to recognize the grandson he loved so dearly.

"I didn't know your father," Gracie admitted. "That was right before my time. However, I know how proud your grandfather was of you."

Hammie's "Thanks" was soft but no less heartfelt for that.

"Life didn't stop the day your father died, Hammie," Bill said, joining them in front of the clock. "You and your brother became his legacy. This clock is just a thing — gears and weights." Bill paused. "What's more, you took that store's old-fashioned charm and added your own welcome to it. Inviting us all out here is part of it."

"Hey, no big deal. Orville wanted to visit the place, and I just had the idea. I don't come out much anymore. Too busy, I guess. This weekend seemed made to order."

"I'm glad you planned it," Gracie told him. "And it meant a lot to Uncle Miltie to be included."

"I guess I was also hoping having the guys around would make this reunion with Orville a bit easier. It surprised me, his deciding to come straight out of the blue like

31

that. And Sherry hasn't been feeling well, not really up to company. Coming out here seemed the perfect solution."

"Why don't you go ahead and tell Gracie your good news — why Sherry's been sick?" Bill said. "I think she'd love to know."

Hammie blushed.

"Sherry's expecting!" Gracie exclaimed. Her voice carried around the room, and now the rest of their friends looked toward the trio standing in front of clock. Hammie had turned a little pink with his revelation. "Umm. . . ."

Gracie hugged him. "Congratulations!"

"I knew it!" Uncle Miltie boasted. "I told the guys as much the other day, when Sherry came out of the office to check receipts with you. She's always a pretty young woman, but she looked practically radiant!"

"When's the baby due?" Gracie wanted to know.

"In late December."

"Have you told Sherry's family?" Gracie remembered they had retired to Florida several years earlier.

"Right before I left Sherry called her mom, so I'm sure they all know by now. We told my great-aunt after church last Sunday. Aunt Polly told everyone at the nursing home that she was expecting her first great-grandniece or nephew, too."

Gracie hugged him again. "Oh, Hammie!"

"This might be the right occasion to re-suscitate that clock," Bill suggested. "In honor of your dad's first grandchild!"

Orville crossed his arms and leaned against the fireplace on the other side of the room. Gracie couldn't help praying that this stony-faced young man would let God into his heart. She hadn't even seen him react to the news. Had Hammie noticed, too? How could he not feel joyful?

Uncle Miltie inspected the clock. "What say we take a look-see? Figure out what's ailing the old fellow!"

Hammie was hesitant. "I don't know. All this time. . . ."

"More than thirty years," Orville gibed from the other side of the room. "Grandpa probably wouldn't like it."

Gracie looked at Hammie. "It's your call."

Hammie decided with a quick nod. Then he took a couple of steps back and allowed the others to gather around the clock.

"Let's you and me get that top," Rocky suggested to Grover, as he tried to figure out how to dismantle the cap piece.

Lester put on his glasses and joined them.

Gracie stood next to Hammie, who'd moved over to the fireplace to join his brother.

"Feels a little like messing with a curse," Orville said under his breath.

Hammie obviously heard him, but chose not to comment.

Gracie couldn't stop herself. "You really think the clock is cursed?"

"I think our family's cursed. My mother was killed on her way out to this place only a few months after my dad died here. And my grandfather kept it like a shrine. Who'd want to come here, with that clock silently screaming at them, daring them to live on? No wonder my mother was depressed. This place would do it to anyone. I'll never figure out why they loved it so much."

She looked thoughtfully at Orville before replying. "Memories, maybe. Sad ones, it's true, but probably many wonderful ones, too. It still makes me feel better to sit in my husband's favorite chair, or hug his pillow at night."

"Yeah, well, not me. I always hated this place. And the rest of Willow Bend!"

Gracie didn't know how to respond. *Lord, help us to love him as You do.*

"I need a dustcloth and a flashlight," Uncle Miltie called out.

Hammie glanced over at his brother as if

to say something, but instead went to fetch the requested items. Despite the friendly clutter, he found both items quickly. Rocky held the flashlight for Uncle Miltie, as Lester positioned himself to examine the works.

"I feel like I'm a part of history," Bill announced. "First, I was the bearer of the good news to Sherry, and now we're starting the clock to honor your child, Hammie!"

"Perfectly providential! It's a beautiful gesture," Gracie agreed, making a mental note to take a gift to Sherry. Undoubtedly, the best place for her purchase would be her best friend Marge Lawrence's gift shop. Marge would adore helping Gracie to pick it out!

Hammie and Sherry Miller were among the best-liked of Willow Bend's young marrieds. Gracie even remembered that Marge and Hammie's mother had been friends. That was before she and El had settled in Willow Bend, but Marge still spoke fondly of Patty Miller, and to this day kept a friendship with Polly Reid, the aunt who'd helped Sam Miller raise the boys after his wife died. Gracie would call Marge with the news as soon as she got home that afternoon.

"These clocks are amazing," Lester marveled. He gently worked at something in the clock. "Well, lookey here!"

"What have you found?" Uncle Miltie asked excitedly, straining to see what Lester was trying to disengage from the gears. Gracie moved for a closer view but was forced to stare at Rocky's broad back.

"I feel like I'm in one of your mystery novels," Rocky told her, turning around and thoughtfully making room.

"Don't need to know anything about clocks, to pluck something out of the gears." Lester held up a small green packet, from which dangled a key attached to a cord.

He wiped the dust off his discovery. "Now, how do you suppose this got in there?"

Gracie couldn't imagine, but she felt her heart beat faster.

Rocky reached to take the key from Lester. "My guess is that it goes to a safe deposit box. Look, there's a number on it — 347. But no other information, no address or name or anything."

"Wait!" Rocky turned it over in his palm. The word *Cassidy* was written in pencil, now faded and barely legible. It meant nothing to any of them.

"Is this what stopped the clock?"

Rocky nodded. "Seems to me the right answer."

Lester moved to inspect the gears where he'd freed the string. "These clocks are sensitive. Get something a hair off plumb, and you've got problems."

"So, why would someone stick a key in a clock case?" Rocky asked no one in particular.

Orville came closer to examine the tidy little packet in Rocky's hand. "It might even be a key to something around the house here. Bank keys have a certain look."

Gracie turned to Hammie. "You don't have any idea who would have put it there?"

Hammie looked bewildered. "I don't know anybody named Cassidy."

"Let me see it," Orville said.

Gracie glanced at Hammie, who nodded absently. "Fine, take a look."

"It could be the key to the box where Grandpa stashed his research notes," Orville told his brother. "I'll just hang on to it in case we turn something up."

"I can't come up with an answer that makes any sense to me," Hammie told Gracie. "Grandpa kept everything important in the safe in his office. He didn't have a bank safety deposit box, at least not that I ever knew about."

"If he had," Rocky commented, "it probably would have been something that turned up in his papers when he died."

"What about your parents?" Gracie asked.

Hammie considered this for a moment. "I can't say for sure. They did spend a lot of time out here."

Orville reached for the key, but Rocky chose to hand it to Hammie. "You knew your grandfather best. I think you're the best person to hold on to it."

"Suit yourself," Orville said. But Gracie saw he wasn't pleased with Rocky's interference.

Gracie studied the pair. It occurred to her, then, that there was more than one mystery in this room begging to be solved. She glanced toward Grover, who'd been silent throughout the discussion of the discovery of the old clock's secret. He looked thoughtful.

It was a strange coincidence, she felt, that he, too, had a past connection to Acorn Lake, and one that was possibly as shot through with emotions as sensitive as the Millers' own were. The sadness he'd revealed when talking about his brother Franklin still haunted his face.

What did it all mean?

3

Gracie had just gotten out of bed and, now dressed, she came face to face with Lester, who greeted her brightly. He was almost too cheery for this early hour. It was barely sunrise, and Gracie had assumed that she'd be the only early riser after their late night around the fireplace.

She'd hoped to get coffee on before the troops arose for another day of fishing. What's more, she intended to be on the road back to Willow Bend soon after that. Even if the fishermen were taking Monday off, she had no intention of doing so.

She looked at the grandfather clock, now missing its face case.

"I got it to work," Lester announced.

"Have you been up all night?"

Lester shook his head. "The answer came to me early this morning. After we'd put it back together last night, and it still didn't work, I decided that it was meant to be silent. Then I thought of what Bill said, and I really wanted to make that clock work, for their baby's sake. That's when I remembered the third weight — the one pulled clear to the top. That would stop it — if it had jumped the hook, that is. I'm hoping that was the only problem."

He motioned her to join him in front of the clock, which was now busily ticking off the minutes. "You know, this was a pretty terrific invention. Think of it, Gracie — a simple oscillating gear system that allows a slowly descending weight on a cord to drive the clockwork at a steady rate."

Gracie stared at him, not knowing how to respond.

"Mechanical clocks were designed in the fourteenth century, almost simultaneously in Italy and Britain. But they weren't popular until after the monks started using them in the monasteries to mark prayer time."

He grinned. "You can appreciate that, I'm sure." Gracie grinned back.

Lester crossed his arms. The old clock ignored them both. "Why, without clocks, the modern notion of productivity wouldn't exist! That's what my dad used to say. He was a watchmaker."

Gracie reached out and rubbed the wooden surface. "I don't think I knew that."

Lester nodded. "I've always loved understanding the way things work. So, I got up this morning, and began to eliminate possibilities. That's the beauty of machines — they're predictable."

Lester placed the top back on the clock. "As long as you pull up the weights, this senior citizen will tick away through the centuries."

"So I guess the key wasn't the problem."

"That's a 'Which came first, the chicken or the egg?' kind of question. Did the key fall in the gears and stop the clock? Or had it simply run down, so that when someone — probably Sam — tried to rewind it, the weight got pulled up too hard? The key would be immaterial, in that case."

"It's just so strange. I haven't been able to get my mind off that key. And yet there's something so sentimental about the clock's having stopped around the time Todd Miller died," Gracie said. "Of course, there's a splendid symmetry to starting the clock in honor of a new generation of Millers. It has such dignity!"

"Yes, that's why I wanted to get it working. Its dignity, as you call it, seemed ready to be restored at last. Any clock that doesn't tell time is undoubtedly pretty embarrassed by the fact." He chuckled.

Gracie's own sense was that the weekend had unfolded as it had to some purpose. Still, it was obvious that more than the clock needed healing.

"I'll make coffee."

Lester grinned. "It's already on. You don't tackle applied science at five in the morning without a little caffeine boost."

After breakfast, the men gathered their gear for another day out on the lake, and Gracie cornered her uncle to say goodbye.

"Thank you, Gracie. I'm sorry that you chased out here for nothing."

"Don't be silly! I was one of the first to hear Hammie's good news. That alone was worth the drive! Not to mention witnessing the rekindling of history — or Miller family history, at any rate. But now I have to get back. I'm catering a luncheon coming up for the Garden Club, and I want to experiment with a new recipe."

She glanced at her watch. "It looks like it's going to be a nice morning for driving. A bit cooler. Being on the road in the sunshine always makes me hopeful — and I'll even get back early enough to provide some exercise for both me and Gooseberry."

"That reminds me of the farmer who walked into the house after chores," Uncle Miltie said with a twinkle. "He sat down at the table and scratched his head. 'What's got you so perplexed?' asked his wife. The answer: 'I'm trying to figure out where I can find all that daylight I saved when I set back the clocks!' "

He laughed, and Gracie shook her head. "What am I to do with you?"

"Just what you already do!" He grinned, raising a bushy eyebrow as he surveyed his companions. "Give me enough nurture so that I'll always have enough energy to tell one more!"

Gracie pretended horror. "I hadn't realized I could be considered an accomplice, what they call an enabler! If I feed you only cold gruel, will you tell fewer jokes?"

"That'd take an injection of pun-icillin!"

"Ouch!"

Uncle Miltie put his arm around her. "You *are* wonderful, Gracie. Have a safe drive! We're all glad you came. That shepherd's pie was magnificent! See you at home!"

She hugged him.

"Can you believe this guy?" Bill Wright joined them now. "Less than twenty-four hours ago, we thought he was a goner, and look at him now!"

Uncle Miltie cleared his throat. "It's a darn sight better to be over the hill than under it." Then he made a shooing motion with his arm. "Go on now, Gracie! We can take care of ourselves!"

"Thanks again for dinner!" Hammie called to her.

"What about the fish? Are you guys going to fillet them and freeze them?" Gracie asked.

"We've got to catch them, first," Rocky told her.

Grover laughed. "If the fish are biting here, it's only each other."

Rocky hugged her goodbye. "Whether we catch anything or not we'll sponsor that fish fry. I think it's a fun idea!"

He scanned the group. "We're entering the final stages of the first annual Acorn Lake Fish-a-thon! Right, guys?"

"Maybe you could stay for it?" Hammie said to Orville. His brother only shrugged.

"I'll even come down from Chicago for the event," Grover told them. "I know a wholesale supplier who might be able to get us a good price on fish."

Uncle Miltie feigned indignation. "Hey, today it's going to be different! My money's on Gravino to reel in the big one."

Gracie, eyebrows raised, shot him a warning glare. "First stop, the shores of Acorn Lake, next thing you know he'll be in Vegas at the slot machines!"

Lester reminded her, "It's all in fun, Gracie. Drive safely!"

The clock chimed the hour, followed by an eerie moment of silence.

Gracie leaned back, allowing the hum of Fannie Mae's ten-year-old engine to put her mind at ease. Mother Parks always said the best way to take the fear out of living was to put faith in the Lord. Gracie concurred. *Lord, thank You for reminding me that all we are, and all we have, are in Your capable care.*

As usual, lists began to form in her mind as the scenery passed by. Cat food for Gooseberry. And a final checklist for the luncheon she was catering for the Garden Club. Cheese for the little biscuits she liked to serve with the ham salad and some jars of bread-and-butter pickles for the relish trays. Oranges and pineapples for the ambrosia.

There was also the return call to her niece. She'd meant to phone Carter right away in response to the rather gloomy-sounding message she'd left on Gracie's answering machine. But then she'd received Bill Wright's urgent summons. Uncle Miltie was fine now, she reminded herself.

Carter would be celebrating a birthday in a few weeks. Now, how old would she be? She and Arlen were nearly the exact same age — just a few months' difference. She smiled at the memory of the two of them indulging in after-supper Monopoly marathons on the front porch, during those long-ago summers when Carter regularly would come down from Chicago.

She decided to call both Carter and Arlen! She missed her son and his family. Manhattan was only a plane flight away, but it felt worlds removed from the peace and beauty that was Willow Bend.

Gracie ached for her grandson terribly. Her visits with him — even their weekly phone calls — made her heart feel as if it were soaring above the clouds. His unpredictable take on the English language alone could bring her delight that lasted through every replay of their conversation to Uncle Miltie, Marge or Pastor Paul. She laughed, remembering Elmo telling her that his mom and dad were his "next to skin."

What a boy he was! How his grandfather would have adored him and how his heart would have soared with hers! Yes, she would call them all that very afternoon! But first there was her walk and the special time she needed to talk things over with God.

The pines lining the road blended with bits of nostalgia and memory as she recalled summer trips to Acorn Lake when Arlen was a boy. El had brought him here to work on his Eagle Scout requirements, Gracie had been so proud of her son and husband when Arlen received the prestigious "God and Country" award. They had been so very close, father and son. She felt a twinge of sadness that the Miller brothers had never really known their father.

She noticed motorboats moored in a rustic marina. El and Rocky had even owned a motorboat together for a while. Thinking of the Miller brothers and Grover again, Gracie thanked God that nothing ever had intruded upon the friendship between her husband and the newspaperman. Since El's death Rocky had become one of her closest friends. Not only did he humor her incorrigible uncle, playing chess and checkers with him and abetting him in his umpteen home-improvement projects, he also genuinely cared about Uncle Miltie.

Her thoughts turned to the previous night. What was behind Grover's sadness? Hammie knew but approached it cautiously for reasons she couldn't discern. And Orville was a young man so lacking in compassion. She lifted all three up to the Lord. It seemed the past was never thoroughly past-tense, but was rather always a filler for the future.

Life was certainly mysterious. It was a good thing Gracie preferred it that way.

"Oh, no!"

She hit the brakes, hard.

4

The deer bolted to the edge of the woods on the other side of the road.

Gracie took several controlled breaths, willing her still-racing heart back to normal. *"Thank You, Lord,"* she whispered from the deepest part of herself. Both she and the animal were unhurt. She sat for a moment, regaining her composure.

The sun pierced the morning fog, creating a stunning spotlight effect on the field in front of her. The deer stood stock-still now beyond the roadside bramble, staring at her.

Gracie climbed out of the car to get a better view. She fondly patted Fannie Mae's dashboard as she did. "Good girl."

A thicket and small stream separated the road from the woods beyond. Gracie slipped on a muddy rock, landing on her knees and scraping her palms. But in front of her stood the deer with two fawns.

Oh, Lord, they are so beautiful! Gracie couldn't take her eyes off the deer, and sat quietly trying not to startle them. Soon, satisfied that she posed no threat, they went back to their grazing. First one bent its head, then the others.

The sun grew warmer as she sat there, washing away the chilly pink and purple tint from the sky, and making the deer's coats shimmer with golden highlights.

"Lord, You are here," she whispered, fully in the moment with her Creator.

After a while, the deer leaped away. Gracie watched as they disappeared from view, and sadness filled her.

"Gracie, you okay?" She started at the sound of a voice behind her.

There was Harry Durant, offering her his hand. The gas-station manager and repair-shop owner seemed to have a positive radar for trouble. His car now was parked in front of hers, facing in the opposite direction.

"A deer darted out in front of Fannie Mae," she told him. "I saw that she had a pair of fawns. I wanted to make sure she was okay."

"Well, Fannie Mae looks none the worse for the encounter. And you seem to have made sure the deer's all right. How about you?"

"A little shook up, but grateful. I could have hit her."

Harry nodded. "Deer can do a lot of damage. Ruin the radiator, take out the windshield. You were lucky."

"Not luck." Gracie glanced heavenward.

He smiled.

"I must look a fright!" she exclaimed, suddenly realizing her hand was bleeding.

"Nothing a hot bath and a Band-Aid won't cure."

Gracie appreciated his kindly tone. Harry Durant could sometimes be brusque, but she knew him to be a kind man.

Harry walked around the front of the car, rubbing his hand on the fender. "She's looking pretty good. When's the last time you had her in for a tune-up?"

Gracie really couldn't remember. El used to handle the car maintenance. "I need one of those reminder notes, like a dentist sends."

Harry made a disgusted grunt as he hunkered down to inspect the grill and underpinnings.

"I didn't hit the deer," Gracie reminded him.

"Just giving the old girl a once-over."

She was guilty of ignoring her car's symptoms until a problem demanded attention, and Harry knew it. But he liked Gracie and appreciated the sympathetic manner she showed to some of the local teenage boys — kids he himself knew needed only the respect of adults as well as encouragement.

He patted Fannie Mae. "You have to pamper these gals. Or ladies, I should say."

"So, what brings you out this way?" Gracie moved to the driver's side of her car.

"Headed to Hammie's place. I had some work to finish, so I couldn't come up with the rest of the gang." He looked at her and suddenly realized where she must have been. "Catering a fishing expedition? That's a new one!"

"I drove out and wound up spending the night." Gracie filled him in on the previous afternoon's events. "As far as I know, they haven't actually caught anything yet."

"Good fishing's just a matter of timing," Harry told her, chuckling. "You have to get there yesterday!"

Gracie laughed. "You must have heard that from Uncle Miltie. But, then, I suppose every fisherman has a bait box filled with jokes."

She slid into the driver's seat. "Thanks for stopping, Harry."

"How about starting her up for me, just to be on the safe side? This isn't exactly the luckiest neck of the woods."

"So Orville Miller says."

But Harry's attention was on the engine. "I'm listening to the valve tappet. Might be one of your lifters aren't pumping up. It's a minor problem, but we ought to take care of it."

Gracie returned to the subject of the Millers. "You probably know about the accidents — Hammie's parents dying within months of each other. His mother was killed on this road."

Harry pulled off his cap, emblazoned with a "Gas-and-Go" logo, and scratched his head. "That was over thirty years ago. Don't remember much more than how bad it shook up the town. They were so young."

Gracie looked out her window at him. "I get the impression there are still unanswered questions."

"Folks make up all kinds of stories when something weird like that happens — a man drowns. A woman who happens to have been married to him soon has a fatal car accident. It's the stuff of campfire tales. So, what's true and what isn't? I don't know."

"Then you've heard the story I just learned about the grandfather clock?"

"Everybody's heard that one. I'm surprised you never heard it before."

Gracie told him Hammie and Sherry's news, and about his decision to fix the clock. Then she described the discovery of the key in the works.

"Thinking of tackling this mystery, Gracie?"

She shrugged. "It does make you wonder who put the key in the clock and why."

"I'd bank on coincidence," Harry said, and paused.

She told him about the jammed weight.

"The story went around that the clock stopped the minute Todd took his last breath. Can't beat that for shivers!" Harry rubbed his chin. "A key in the works takes it back to the realm of the real. If you ask me, seems more likely someone stuck that key there for safekeeping. No one actually knows for sure if that clock *did* stop the day Todd Miller died — but it makes for a great spooky story! You know, like that old show *The Twilight Zone*."

Gracie waited. She could tell there was more he wanted to say.

"You know Hammie's Aunt Polly, don't you?" Harry now asked. "Of course, she's Orville's Aunt Polly, too. She's out at Pleasant Haven, and would probably dearly love company. She might be able to satisfy your curiosity. Besides, you two have something in common. She drove an elderly Impala until she stopped driving altogether. Now there was a Chevy with an attitude!"

His expression turned quizzical. "Wonder what she did with the old girl? If you happen to think of it, ask her."

Harry patted the Cadillac's dark blue roof. "This one's a spunky Detroit dame, I'll give her that. You ever want to sell her, let me know."

They chatted a couple of minutes more about old cars, finally getting around to Hammie's vintage Ford pickup.

"I'll take his old classic to that sporty import his brother drives. Orville breezed into town the other day, and pulled into my place, looking for me to be impressed."

She was uncertain what to say.

"I don't know what to make of his coming back after all these years. Trouble for Hammie, if I don't miss my guess."

"Let's hope not."

Harry nodded, none too convinced. "Every family's got to have a black sheep, I guess. Orville's theirs."

"Every black sheep has a Savior," Gracie told him. "None of us are too far gone for the Lord."

He looked at her without comment. Smiling gravely, she reminded him that God buried sins in an unmarked grave, so they couldn't be identified.

"That's more than we can say for humans. We seem to get a kick out of reminding folks of their failings," Harry replied. "I try to avoid gossip, myself. I take a man at his worth. But sometimes, I just get a bad feeling. Orville took advantage of Hammie before. I'd sure hate to see him get away with it again."

"What do you mean?"

Harry tugged at his hat. "Maybe it means nothing, but that car is rented."

"How do you know?"

"The gauges weren't reading right, so he asked me to look at it. I had to see the registration. It's not his own, all right." He met her gaze. "What do you think he really wants?"

Gracie had no idea. "Well, he says he's retrieving his grandfather's journals — something about hoping to duplicate a formula for a hybrid alfalfa."

"I can't imagine that guy ever getting his hands dirty. Well, physically, anyway. Old Sam Miller knew that. That's why he left the store to Hammie."

It had seemed fitting for Hammie to inherit the old-fashioned agricultural supply store that his grandfather had founded. Miller's Feed Store was known throughout Mason County for its hospitality, and its never-empty big blue enamel coffee pot. There was simply no way to imagine its changing in any way. Orville Miller as its proprietor could never have worked.

"The old man did right by Orville, though. Or, at least, so I've been told. Orville took his inheritance up front. Went off to find his fortune back East. I heard he gambled it away and that the old man had to bail him out a couple of times. That's why he left the rest to Hammie. I think the cabin and farm are still in both their names, though. Maybe the old man was holding out hope for Orville."

"Orville says he has land in Pennsylvania," she remembered. She decided it was only right to give him the benefit of the doubt. "Hammie seems quite proud of him."

Harry shrugged. "I'd like to see Orville turn it around, for Hammie's sake. Old Sam Miller was hard on those boys, but he loved them both. I know it hurt him that Orville insisted on being given the entire inheritance from his parents. Then he up and took off, with no word for years. Maybe he's come around."

"I didn't know Sam Miller very well," Gracie admitted. "But my husband admired him. He said he was a fair businessman."

"He was a stickler for honesty, and for a good day's work. When he still tinkered with feed corn, I used to work for him pulling the tassels off the cornstalks. Didn't cotton to slackers. I think that's where he and Orville came to blows. Orville was a lot like his dad that way."

Harry stuck his hands in his pockets. "Todd Miller was older than me, but I remember hearing about him as a jock. One who liked carousing with his buddies. He was always wanting to move on to the next thing, impatient, you might say. Too much so to stick out the long days of running a feed store business."

"I'll bring Fannie Mae in bright and early tomorrow," she promised him.

"Not too early! I got some serious fishing to catch up on, so I don't figure getting back before lunch. My part-time guy will be there to pump gas, but I like to supervise the shop. That's my name on the door — and a man can't be too careful with his good name."

"Well, I wish you luck. I hope they're biting for you!"

"Not luck." He grinned.

"A guardian angel?"

"Right lure." He winked.

She waved. "Enjoy yourself. And, Harry, look out for my uncle, will you? I don't want anymore phone calls!"

"Sure thing, Gracie!"

The day had started off unsettling, and continued to be unsettling. But such days were best handled with prayer. And she had a bit more than an hour still to go before she hit the outskirts of Willow Bend.

I'm listening, Lord.

5

Just as Gracie was turning her key in the lock, Marge Lawrence appeared beside her. "I got your message. Is Uncle Miltie okay? The fact that he's not with you seems to be a clue of some sort, but then I'm not the detective you are."

Gracie filled her friend in on his speedy recovery as they entered the kitchen. Gooseberry hopped down from his perch on the window sill to sit at her feet, his tail swishing. She bent to scratch his head. "You were worried about him, weren't you, old boy?"

The pumpkin-colored cat licked a paw and began washing himself.

"I think he's trying to tell us that, as far as he's concerned, everything's back to normal." Gracie laughed.

"Hmmm."

"Gooseberry may be thinking 'business as usual,' but I'm going to be keeping an eye on him when he gets home tomorrow."

"Just don't let him see you doing it!"

"He may have acted a little indignant that I drove out there, but I think, secretly, he was relieved. Dr. Wright says he's as strong as a horse . . ."

Marge finished her sentence, ". . . if a horse lived into his eighties!"

Uncle Miltie and Marge usually enjoyed a mock adversarial relationship, but that was only on the surface. They cared for each other with deep affection.

A few years earlier, after the death of his wife, Uncle Miltie had come to live with Gracie for what they had originally planned as a couple of months of recovery. He'd arrived depressed, lonely and relying on a walker to get around. Marge and Rocky, along with Gracie, had prodded him to get on with life. Her best friend and next-door neighbor simply had refused to let him feel sorry for himself and had encouraged him to become involved with the community. Rocky, for his part, had accepted the role of Laurel to Uncle Miltie's Hardy, acting as sidekick and apprentice handyman.

"Well, probably no one ever expired with a rod in their hand, at least not in a little lake called Acorn. I mean, deep-sea fishing's something altogether different — but there aren't any sharks in Indiana!"

Gracie laughed with her. "I don't know what I would do without him! He's one of a kind!"

Marge declared, "I hope to have his energy when I hit his age, that's all I can say!"

Gracie now explained. "It turns out that it was some kind of fool challenge on who could catch the most fish, with Uncle Miltie acting as self-appointed cheerleader and referee."

"With one overconfident newspaperman hollering loudly, too, if I don't miss my guess." Marge opened the refrigerator door.

"The iced tea's at the back," Gracie said, second-guessing her.

"Want me to go out and grab a sprig or two of mint?"

Gracie nodded. "Perfect!"

Marge poured two glasses. "They're not coming home until tomorrow, right? How about we go out for supper after choir practice tonight?"

"Okay, but remember, we've got that meeting, first — Barb wants to show us the bells, remember?"

Marge's eyes widened. "That's right!"

Eternal Hope's choir director had responded to the choir's new enthusiasm by asking a friend in Avery to lend them her set for a week or so. Barb was hoping to stir up enough interest among the congregation to get the funding for their bell choir. But many other projects also had claims on the community's checkbooks: wondrously stirring as the bells were, they were, nonetheless, still a luxury.

"White gloves and brass bells. Elegant." Marge struck a sophisticated pose. "I can hardly wait to try them."

Gracie agreed. She, too, was looking forward to trying her hand at the bells. There was something awe-inspiring in the syncopation, that perfect blending of timing and tone. She was proud of Barb for taking the risk. It would not only be more work for her as director, but a real job to convince the less musically inspired trustees and members that the purchase was worth the cost.

Before Marge left, Gracie filled her in on all the adventures at the Miller cabin.

"That's wonderful!" Marge was thrilled to know about the Miller baby on the way. She giggled at the notion of a community fish fry fundraiser.

"It does sound like fun — but can they really catch that much? And how would they keep the fish? An event like that needs planning."

Gracie laughed. "I'm not sure they can catch enough to feed themselves minnows on crackers, and the town would starve if they waited for an Acorn Lake feast. The idea's clever, though, and it came up out of the blue."

"You know, it could be the kickoff for a fundraising campaign. Maybe the choir from Avery could even come play at the dinner, as a tempting sample of what we hope to sound like one day."

"I think you're right, Marge. Hooray for our guys! Now, if they can just catch some fish!"

Gracie's friend sat down at the table, resting her chin on her knuckles, and sighed. "I haven't been up to Acorn Lake in years. You probably remember, Hammie's mother and I were friends. I'd go up to help her with the boys from time to time when Todd was out of town — which was a lot, particularly in the spring and early summer. His sales job took him to farm shows and county fairs. But he did love to fish!"

"I must say, I'm curious to know more about the family. Hammie's a lovely man, and he and Sherry have all their happiness ahead of them now. But Orville's a mystery to me, and Harry Durant certainly doesn't trust him."

Marge snorted politely. "You remember their Aunt Polly? I know only too well how she used to worry herself sick about that boy. I'll bet she still does."

"She was an art teacher, wasn't she?"

Marge nodded. "Orville had a streak of mischief that kept her on her toes. She knew he'd get Hammie blamed for stuff he'd done himself — Orville, that is. Polly would suspect the true culprit, but Hammie always covered for his brother. They were as different as day and night."

"That's often the case," Gracie conceded, remembering how different she and her own brother had been. She thought of his daughter Carter, and that unhappy-sounding message she'd left on Gracie's answering machine. Usually so cheery, Carter's voice this time sounded cheerless and thus very out of character for the highly competent young lawyer.

Lord, I hope nothing is wrong.

"You okay?" Marge was staring at her.

Silently, she thanked God for the love He spread over friends and family, always there beside them. "I'm sorry, my mind was on something else."

"The key? Do you really think that's what

stopped the clock?" Marge now switched subjects herself.

Gracie understood something important had been discovered out there at Acorn Lake. She only wished she knew what. Moreover, the question remained whether it was any of her business. "I prefer to believe the clock succumbed to a broken heart."

"There's so much pain surrounding those deaths," Marge said softly. "You just can't imagine. It's there to this day, even." She sighed.

Gracie sensed that it was not the time to probe.

Gracie managed to reach Carter on her cell phone. Her niece sounded exhausted.

"I hope you're getting enough rest — and making time for church, dear. That's the best medicine when your stress levels hit the danger zone."

Gracie heard Carter draw in her breath. *Just give her a little nudge, Lord. She hasn't meant to lose her way.*

They made small talk for a few minutes, but Gracie sensed that Carter was preoccupied. She was unsure what to ask, hating to pry. "It's wonderful to talk to you, but did you call for a special reason?"

"No reason."

But the silence on the other end contradicted this assertion. Gracie would have to wait Carter out.

"Everything's so politicized here," her niece suddenly burst out. "It's crazy. Sometimes I feel like my boss is simply notching his belt like some gunslinger. It's all about winning! But these aren't just cases, they're people, too. Often bad people, but people, just the same. Oh, Aunt Gracie, I'm so frustrated! Sometimes I just want to give up law. Go off and join the Peace Corps, or something."

Gracie didn't know how to respond.

"I'm sorry, I'm just venting."

"Have you talked to him about this? You're working hard and probably not getting enough rest. I can imagine you have little time for social activity." Gracie realized that she was trying to offer solutions when all Carter needed was someone to listen.

"That's not it, Aunt Gracie. I love my job! That's what scares me — I love it *too* much. It's great to win! So it isn't really my boss's ambition, or our conviction record that bothers me, it's my own drive. I don't want to become obsessed, always looking for the way to come out on top. I want to prosecute the bad guys, sure, but I want to be sure I keep my heart."

Carter was quiet for a long minute. "I'm so confused."

Gracie couldn't help but remember Carter as a teenager in braces debating long and earnestly with her Uncle El. Gracie recalled the day she'd announced that she'd passed the bar exam. It always had seemed certain Carter was born to be a lawyer — but now, could it be that Carter herself was thinking otherwise?

"I'm going to be thirty," Carter now said. She paused. The sentence seemed to hang there in the air. "I told Mom to go on her trip to the Holy Land, that I'd be fine on my birthday without her. I know it's stupid but, Aunt Gracie, now that she's not here, it does bother me."

Gracie wished she could give her niece a hug. "Where would the world be without you, Carter? Without any of us, really? God created us each special, to do wonderful things. And that means birthdays are special, too."

"Aunt Gracie, you're so great! I guess it's just one of those adult passages — my confusion, I mean. I ought to have some idea what I want to do with the rest of my life. Do I want to stay with the district attorney? Do I want to be a litigator all my life? Do I want to get married and have children?"

"Pray," came off Gracie's lips as easily as the love that filled her heart for her accomplished niece. "God knows what is best for you, dear. Talk it over with Him."

Gracie could feel Carter smile. "You think God can find me a date for my thirtieth birthday?"

Gracie laughed. "Why don't you come spend it with me? I'll bake a white coconut cake, with that creamy icing you used to like so much."

"Sounds decadent."

"We could rent a couple of those movies you've probably been trying to find the time to see."

Carter laughed. "That would be fun! We could curl up in flannel pajamas, just like when I used to come to your house as a girl. Remember *Anne of Green Gables* and *Little Women*? How many times did we watch them?"

"Enough to drive El and Arlen from the house." Gracie chuckled. "Those are special memories. I always did want a little girl."

"And me a brother." Carter laughed. "Most of the time, that is. My cousin was too fond of snakes, frogs and other gross-out creatures."

"Why don't you come?" Gracie made up her mind, already planning the menu for a birthday celebration.

"I'd love to . . . but, right now, I'm swamped."

"All the more reason to get away."

"I miss you," Carter confessed. "And Willow Bend. And Uncle Miltie. Gooseberry, too."

Gracie glanced toward heaven, uttering a humble plea. *Please, You know she needs a vacation. And I'd love to see her.*

"I'm praying that God clears the way," she told her niece.

"Between you and God, I guess my boss doesn't stand a chance," Carter laughed.

6

Marge slipped on a pair of white cotton gloves and picked up one of the brass choir bells on loan from the church in Avery. She grinned at Gracie and giggled. "I feel like a schoolgirl."

Gracie shared in her excitement, taking the position beside her at the table covered with black velvet.

"Awesome!" Amy Cantrell came up behind them. Eternal Hope's youngest choir member brought her inimitable sparkle to the choir loft. A gifted soprano, Amy embraced every musical endeavor with passion, and usually managed in the process to irritate the diva who saw her as a rival. As if on cue, Estelle Livett scurried down the aisle.

"Be careful! Don't pick up the bells without gloves and tarnish them!" she called out querulously.

Their choir director turned to face her. "Thank you, Estelle. But everyone has already heard my instructions."

Marge wiggled her white-clad fingers at Estelle.

"You can't take any chances, you know. We'll end up trying to come up with money to pay for the ones we borrowed before we get any of our own!"

Estelle stopped short of bulldozing Gracie down. "I tried to get here early, thinking you'd benefit from my advice."

"We might, indeed, Estelle." Barb's tone was amazingly patient. Estelle could be so very exasperating to them all. Barb was an accomplished organist and pianist, and had had experience with bell choirs in college. It was plain to see she was thrilled at the prospect of starting one at Eternal Hope. Now, if they could only come up with the necessary funds!

Rick Harding appeared beside Gracie. "Wow!"

"My feelings exactly!" Amy told him. "Can you believe we're going to make music with these?"

"I've always loved bell choirs," Rick told them. "Perfect timing and fluid motion — choreography for the eyes and ears."

Marge gave her small bell a tinkle. "My

goodness, Rick, that's practically poetry."

"Well, I can't play a musical instrument." He picked up one of the larger bells, and gave it a gentle shake. "I took piano lessons as a child, but my teacher said it was a waste of her time and my mother's money. Think there's any chance I can learn to make music with these?"

"If you're as good with them as you are with that tenor voice of yours, then your long-ago failure as a boy pianist will soon be the stuff of legend!" Gracie joked.

"I can play piano," Marge told them. "But I wish I'd pursued music more seriously. The truth is, I was more interested in boys than the discipline it took to be a first-class musician."

Marge played a chord combination. "The bell choir will be my chance to use that music training again."

"I begged out of a meeting at the fire hall for this opportunity," Rick told them, caressing a large bell. "I wouldn't miss trying my hand at this for anything."

Rick was also a volunteer with the local emergency services team. But second only to his family — his wife Comfort and precious little daughter Lillian — music was his passion. Always gracious with his talent, always generous and giving, he was a true hero to his fellow choir members.

"Do you really think we might get a set of our own?" he asked Barb. "It's pretty exciting!"

"I know," Marge teased him. "But don't have a heart attack there! Calm down! We need you still in the choir loft."

Rick laughed. "Don't worry! I'm planning to live a long and healthy life. Comfort and my sweet baby daughter wouldn't have it any other way. As wonderful as heaven will be, this tenor is looking forward to singing at his grandchildren's weddings! And learning to play the bells, besides!"

Rick and his wife seemed to have found the perfect balance between their career aspirations and parenting. They'd relocated from the big city to Willow Bend looking for a family-friendly community, and had embraced the members of Eternal Hope as kin. Gracie secretly wished Arlen and Wendy one day would follow the same path and return home.

"This is just too cool!" Rick said, caressing a bell with gloved hands. "When Barb suggested it, I could barely hold myself back."

"You didn't hold yourself back!" Barb reminded him. "You practically danced on the piano when I made the announcement that my friend from Avery was lending us this set."

Gracie watched her choir mates with pleasure.

"It's like a dream come true," Rick said. "A bell choir! I just have to say it again — too cool."

"Bells are very expensive," Barb reminded him.

"God is sufficient!" Rick grinned.

Actually, the funds were already available, or, at least, so Pastor Paul was fond of saying. The trouble was, it was a matter of convincing the saints in the pews to part with them. "You, Rick Harding, are the perfect person to help spread the word! Willow Bells, that's what we have to convince them of — Willow Bells!"

Marge now turned to Gracie. "Tell them what Uncle Miltie and Les Twomley have planned. I think it's a great way to kick off the, *um,* Willow Bells campaign."

The fish fry idea was enthusiastically received — but then any event that promised delicious food was always popular in Willow Bend! Rick, meanwhile, was suggesting that for the occasion they not only utilize the choir, but also his newly organized barbershop quartet.

"Bill Wright sings with us, by the way," he

told Gracie, who'd mentioned to him her emergency rescue mission to Acorn Lake.

"You know, we could even organize a Sweet Adeline group as well," Barb said. "I've always wanted to try something like that."

Marge clapped her hands. "Wow! It's coming together wonderfully. Now, if those guys can just catch some fish!"

Rick laughed. "Fish or no fish, they've caught the spirit, and we have to love them for that!"

"Count me in," said Estelle. "I could help you direct, Barb."

Barb glanced at Gracie. Gracie raised an eyebrow, but sweetly. Estelle was overbearing, it was true, but Gracie knew she loved music every bit as much as Barb did.

"Amy dear, you can be part of the Sweet Adeline choir." Estelle seized her opportunity and began issuing commands. "We'll use Marybeth, of course. And, Gracie, we count on you and —"

She paused to stare haughtily at Marge. "My dear, those earrings are a little distracting, don't you think? What are they, anyway?"

Marge touched her dangling cluster of silver and gold animals. "They represent endangered species, and you know I'd never wear them at a performance!"

"Black dresses, and sensible jewelry. Gracie, you might want to tone down that red hair. It's the complete sense of total harmony that makes any group of Adelines come together as they should."

Gracie bit her lip. *Lord, help me see her as You do.*

Marge leaned close and whispered, "Where do you get your patience?"

"Practice."

Marge shook her head.

"The wonderful thing about patience is that it not only goes a long way," Gracie told her. "The more you use, the more you seem to get."

Barb stood helplessly chewing her lip, as Estelle went on and on about details of their upcoming performance. It was as if she'd had the idea for years instead of only hearing about it minutes before.

"Let's not turn on the fryers before we have the fish. I mean, perhaps we're getting ahead of ourselves," Barb pointed out. "It all still has to be approved."

She suggested that Gracie get the particulars from Rocky and her uncle, then run it by Pastor Paul. Gracie agreed to do so before their next choir rehearsal.

Finally, Barb waved her baton. "My

friends! Let us begin!" It was 6:59 and choir practice began faithfully at 7:00 p.m. on the dot. Always.

It was a challenging session, as Barb set them a new and rather difficult piece. But all understood it would be worth it when they sang it to the Lord. *Of course, You're here with us now, Lord, and our mistakes are as precious to You as our triumphs.*

Gracie happily told Barb as they put away their music, "Choir practice is one of my favorite blessings."

"I know. It makes even the worst day better. I know I fret over little things, letting them get the best of me. I forget how blessed I am, especially with good friends."

Barb looked at Gracie with affection. "Funny, how easily we forsake our blessings for our troubles."

Marge was talking once more to Rick about the fundraiser when Gracie got to the parking lot. While she waited for her friend to finish the conversation, her mind went over all she'd learned that afternoon.

Marge cleared her throat. "Earth to Gracie! You ready to go?"

"I suspect your mind keeps switching back to the Acorn Lake mystery," Marge told her as they opened the car doors. "I've been thinking about it, too. Not that key, so much, but how the past is never really the past. There was something I wanted to tell you this afternoon. . . ."

She glanced around, calling goodbye to Barb and Rick. "I'll tell you over dinner."

Celestial City, the local Chinese restaurant, was almost deserted at this hour. They ordered fried rice and moo shu pork, with soup and egg rolls to start. Marge, while they waited for their food, began to talk to Gracie about her friendship with Patty Miller.

They'd been particularly close in high school, until Patty started dating Todd shortly after they graduated.

"I married my first husband, and Patty and Todd married shortly after. But then they had children, so we drifted apart for a while. They bought her parents' house in Avery when her father was transferred out west. And we didn't see each other much until after Todd died."

Marge paused. "I knew how hard it was to go on alone, because by that time I was on my own again. We grew close during those months right after Todd's death. They hadn't been getting along, and had had a big fight right before he left town. The unresolved anger between them made his sudden passing all the worse.

"She was depressed, Gracie, but by Christmas she seemed better. Then, one night, I got a call from her. She was really upset. She'd overheard a couple of women talking about her in the beauty parlor. That was a couple of nights before she took off for the cabin. She was killed in a one-car accident on the way out there. The weather turned bad, and the roads had become slippery."

Gracie reached over to squeeze her friend's hand.

"They called it an accident, but she was *so* upset. I know! I had to wonder if her mental state had something to do with it." Marge paused, looking unhappy. "What she overheard was gossip about her and Franklin Wills."

Gracie didn't know how to respond.

"It was all my fault." Marge's voice now was barely audible. "I was with her one weekend when Franklin stopped by at her house. I saw them sitting together in the garden, holding hands for a moment."

"You confronted her?"

"Far worse. I'm sure I played a part in spreading the rumors. I told someone else what I'd seen. I never mentioned to you anything about any of this because you never knew Patty."

They sat quietly for a few moments, Gracie watching her friend in silent sympathy until she was again ready to speak.

Marge wiped her eyes. "I should have gone straight to Patty — given her an opportunity to explain. I didn't. Instead, I asked a mutual friend for advice. Apparently, we were overheard."

"Of course, it wasn't true," Gracie guessed.

"Of course not!"

Marge closed her eyes, as if remembering. "Franklin had simply gone to her to offer help. He told me as much at her funeral. I don't think he ever got over what happened. He sold his cabin and never looked back."

"Patty was kind to everyone," Marge said, shaking her head in disbelief. "She was a lot like you, Gracie. She made every day count. And she had a strong, loving relationship with the Lord." A tear ran down her cheek.

Marge met her gaze. "I will never stop feeling ashamed of what I did. Now, it's all coming back to haunt me."

"I'm sure she forgives you. And I *know* God does. And as for being the source of the rumors, you can't be sure. It seems to have been a very strange set of circumstances."

Marge offered a wan smile. "Thanks. I don't know what it has to do with the key, or the Miller brothers, for that matter. But it feels good to get it off my chest."

They sat without speaking for a few moments more as Gracie lifted her friend in silent prayer. *Lord, You are so gracious, forgiving us even before we recognize the need, loving us in spite of our weakness, and seeing us as the people we can become.* "Amen," she said aloud.

Marge said softly, "Thank you, Lord, for my friend Gracie."

Gracie looked at her with affection — and lingering concern.

"I've never told anyone else — until now," Marge sighed. "I've just been so ashamed."

They embraced.

Gracie popped in a gospel CD and donned her headphones. More than good exercise, prayer walking was an hour of precious fellowship with the Lord. What had begun years ago as an exercise in grief management had become the most rewarding part of her day.

She looked forward to walking with God, sharing with Him both her joys and her concerns for those friends and neighbors who came to her attention along the way. This morning, Marge came first to mind.

Her friend had suffered more than her

share of pain, with marriages ending in death or divorce, and no children. Now Marge's mother's health was deteriorating rapidly, and her care was a daily concern. Marge Lawrence was loyal to a fault, and the possibility of her having betrayed anyone would obviously be a permanent wound.

Why was it that rumors seemed the one thing that got thicker as they spread? Poor Marge, she'd learned the hardest way that even well-intentioned words can get twisted and end up bringing harm.

Gooseberry darted from her side into a clump of bushes, just as a squadron of squawking birds zoomed down to drive him from their turf.

Gracie's neighbor Betsy Griswold looked up from deadheading her flowers as the large orange cat emerged into the yard from the bushes. "Well, hello, Gooseberry!"

"How's Uncle Miltie?" she then asked Gracie. "I haven't seen him for a few days!" Gracie filled her in on the perils of the Acorn Lake excursion.

"Hammie Miller is such a kind man. You've heard their news, right?"

"Yes, I have," Gracie told her. "It's lovely, isn't it?"

Next Betsy mentioned that Orville was

back in town. "According to Sherry, he called Hammie one night, saying he was on his way, and the next day he was on their doorstep."

Gracie merely shook her head. Everything she learned about Orville Miller made him more puzzling.

"He didn't trouble to offer any explanation of where he's been these last years. He just turned up expecting his brother to take him in, no questions asked. I suppose that's what family is for, but still. . . ."

"I don't remember Orville very well," Gracie told her. "Hammie was always the kid behind the counter when I went in there."

"Orville's a cold fish. End of story. He didn't want any part of the business, didn't even have the decency to come home for his grandfather's funeral. Sherry said he was out of the country at the time, but you would think he would have raced back when he heard. Makes you wonder what he wants now." Betsy's tone was cynical.

"People do change." Gracie still preferred to be generous. Innocent until proven guilty — it was the right system and she'd stick to it.

"I suppose you're right. But Hammie more than deserves his slice of happiness.

I'd hate to see Orville put a damper on what should be such a happy time for Hammie and Sherry. He's been searching through his grandfather's papers, probably looking for a loophole that'll bring him more cash."

Gracie felt her stomach knot. No one seemed to trust Orville. She really had no reason to be involved, but felt that, somehow, the Lord wanted her to stay with the mystery until it was solved. Otherwise, why had so many pieces of the puzzle made themselves known in her presence?

The Marge angle seemed to create an even more pressing need for resolution — she was Gracie's best friend, after all, and her spirit was sorely troubled by her connection to the Miller tragedy.

But was Gracie only fooling herself, rationalizing old-fashioned nosiness with a misguided sense of mission?

She hoped not.

7

A banging and clanging heralded an outburst of boisterous laughter. Gooseberry jumped from his perch on the window sill and scurried for safety under the table just as the door burst open.

"We're home!" Uncle Miltie announced. The scent of three-day-old dead fish wafted into the kitchen with him.

Rocky appeared behind him, looking the worse for wear. Unshaven and uncombed, he sported a neon-bright shiner that ringed his left eye in purplish-yellow. Tracks of a scabby brush-burn extended across the same cheekbone.

"What happened to you?" Gracie reached out for his cheek, but Rocky dodged her touch, dismissing her concern with a wave of his hand.

"Battle scars." Uncle Miltie set down his

small cooler of provisions.

"Old Hammerhead put up quite a fight," Grover said, bringing up the rear.

"And won!" Uncle Miltie chuckled.

Rocky just grunted, sending his friends into a fit of mocking laughter. Gracie's heart went out to him.

"Did you put something on it?" She tried to get a closer look. "I'll get the antiseptic."

"There was a doctor in the house, re-member?" Uncle Miltie sniffed the air. "What smells so good?"

Gracie turned her attention to the pan of lemon bars that had just emerged from the oven. "Dessert for the Garden Club lun-cheon." She wagged a finger, anticipating the pleas of the ravenous fishermen. "No sampling!"

"But I almost perished from the heat!" Uncle Miltie reminded her piteously.

"Perished from his own cooking is more like it." Grover stepped forward to check out the lemon bars. "*Umm,* they do look good."

The FBI agent looked the most present-able of the trio, in a bulky cable knit sweater and jeans.

"I'm a pretty mean cook, if I do say so my-self," Uncle Miltie declared.

"Yeah, for punishment he gave us sec-onds," Rocky told her.

"He burns the toast so we won't notice the coffee," Rocky added. It was an old routine.

"Thank goodness for fire extinguishers!" Uncle Miltie was definitely enjoying himself.

"You would have been proud of me, Gracie." Her uncle now took a breath, savoring his upcoming punch line. "I delivered the chicken on a wing and a prayer." He cackled delightedly. "On a wing and a prayer — get it?"

Grover groaned. "Would that there'd been leftovers of that delicious shepherd's pie!"

Rocky put his hand on Uncle Miltie's shoulder. "Of course, none of the rest of us volunteered for the job, so who are we to complain, right?"

Gracie started to say something but Grover broke in. "I've got to say, Gracie, your uncle's a wizard in the kitchen. He can make fish taste just like an old shoe."

"Fish?" Uncle Miltie exclaimed. "That was an old shoe! Gravino let the fish get away!"

"I can see it now." Grover spanned his arm envisioning the headline in the *Mason County Gazette*. "Editor leads fish bucket break-out!"

They broke into laughter, causing Rocky to glare at them.

"Will somebody *please* tell me what happened?" Gracie stifled her laughter.

"Remember that fishing challenge we told you about? Well, we had a rematch the next day. Only Gravino didn't hook the big one, his partner Hammie did." Grover grinned at his old friend. "Ahab here, he goes to help pull it in, and proceeds to knock over the container with the day's entire catch."

Uncle Miltie started to laugh again. "You should have seen it, Gracie! The fish were hopping, and we were grabbing, all of them slipping our grip and flying back into the water."

"It's not funny!" Rocky clamped his lips shut in disgust. "Your uncle clubbed me with the bucket, just as Hammie reeled in his fish. I was blindsided!"

"Yeah, but that's not all!" Grover went on. "Rocky comes up out of the water only to get hit in the face by the big one — Old Hammerhead, himself."

Gracie stared. "It was the biggest lake fish I'd ever seen. Hammie had it hooked but couldn't keep hold of it. Rocky's trying to crawl back in the boat to help him, and in all the commotion, Moby Minnow jumps the hook. Leaving them holding the empty bucket. And Gravino wearing a wet suit!"

Gracie leaned back against the counter, holding her sides. If fishing was this much fun, why had she never tried it?

"This reminds me," Uncle Miltie said, eyes dancing, "a man goes into a fancy restaurant and orders a lobster, see. When the waiter brings him one with a broken claw, he asks what happened, and the waiter tells him that the crustacean was in a fight. So the man says — are you ready for this?"

He paused. " 'Okay, then go back and get me the winner!' "

"Aaagh!" cried Grover. "In all my years in the Bureau, I don't know of anyone on the Most Wanted list who could clear a room faster than you!"

"So, how about those lemon bars?" Uncle Miltie asked brightly.

"Lucky for you, I made extras. But I'm going to fix us some lunch first." Gracie shot her uncle a playful grin. "I'm sure you're *all* hungry."

"Your uncle and Rocky have been raving about your cooking," Grover told her. "And I have to admit that shepherd's pie was pretty memorable!

"For what you guys paid, you got a bargain." Uncle Miltie laughed. "I had a lot of practice doing KP in my army days."

Grover looked at Gracie. "He's the life of the party, isn't he?"

"That he is!"

Uncle Miltie was basking in the attention. But Gracie knew him well and could see he was showing signs of exhaustion. She bent to kiss her uncle. "I'm glad to have you home," she said simply.

As she fixed them sandwiches, Rocky made himself at home and started a pot of coffee.

"The real reason that we came home early was because Hammie got a worrying call from his wife," Uncle Miltie told her.

Rocky sensed Gracie's alarm. "Bill didn't think it was serious, but he was going to check in on her this afternoon."

"Hammie said he'll phone you afterward," Uncle Miltie told her. "We knew you'd be pretty worried once you heard."

"You can set the angels to praying," Rocky said, and Gracie for once saw he meant it.

She sent a prayer of love and healing in the direction of the Millers' house, making a note to double the recipe for the cheeseburger loaf she was planning for supper.

Now Rocky asked, "So, what do we make of Lester's little discovery?"

Gracie glanced at him. All the fish tales had distracted her.

"The key in the clock," he reminded her. "Orville never gave up on it. He kept on bugging Hammie to give it to him to hold onto. They didn't manage to find any of the journals Orville was looking for, and Hammie said he didn't think they would."

Gracie thought for a moment. "You don't think there are any records?"

"Oh, there might be records, but Hammie doesn't remember the journals. And, judging by the way Orville rifled through those boxes of papers, he was looking for something very specific. If you ask me, he didn't seem to have the slightest bit of interest in the old man's books on agriculture."

"So, what do you think he's really looking for?"

Rocky munched on a pickle slice. "Maybe whatever that key opens. He sure seemed obsessed with it. Brought it up a half-dozen times in the course of the weekend."

"Seems to me the man must know something he's not telling," Uncle Miltie interjected.

"Kind of reminds me of that Bible story," Rocky mused. "The dad gives his kid his inheritance up front, and the kid squanders it."

"The prodigal son," Gracie suggested.

Rocky nodded. "But the older brother is the stooge in this story."

"Perhaps Hammie is responding in the model of his heavenly Father," Gracie pointed out. "It's a story about forgiveness and reconciliation."

Rocky shook his head, smiling. "Leave it to you, Gracie, to see the silver lining — or the cream filling in the crustiest of us, as you're fond of saying. But frankly, my dear, Orville's just a heck of a hard guy to like."

"He's a got a chip on his shoulder the size of a two-by-four," Uncle Miltie added.

Nonetheless, Gracie thought, she would continue to pray for him, and for Hammie, too. "I would like to think that time has softened whatever anger was between them. Hammie is certainly making a brotherly effort. Perhaps we just should give Orville a chance. More time. Whatever."

"Newspaper work has hardened me to reality. People don't usually change. Once a bad egg, always a stinker."

Gracie had her own thoughts about this. *Lord, I know in every way and in my deepest being that that is not what You believe.*

"Oh, by the way," Rocky said, changing the subject. "Cassidy is a little place an hour or so west of here."

"And how did you find that out?"

"I remembered," Grover said. "I thought it sounded familiar at the time, but I travel so much with the FBI that I couldn't be sure. Later that night, I remembered that Franklin used to go fishing with Todd near Cassidy. They always vied to show each other great new fishing holes."

"Perhaps Todd put the key in the clock," Gracie now thought out loud. "Maybe he rented a safety deposit box in that town for some reason — possibly to leave something for safekeeping while he was traveling."

Rocky shrugged. "Well, it's a funny co-incidence, we thought. And it still might be a last name, for all we know."

"Maybe there's a treasure waiting for the person who figures out the mystery," Uncle Miltie proposed teasingly.

Gracie saw it was possible they were creating a mystery where none existed. "There's a chance, too, that the key unlocked its treasure long ago. Safety deposit keys are given in duplicate, at least that's my experience. That one may have been the extra."

"It's a possibility," Rocky agreed. "And it could have been left there for no reason. Sam Miller was a collector. The guy seemed to save everything, so the key could even be a forgotten piece of memorabilia."

"Yeah, but it was hidden in such an odd spot!" Uncle Miltie countered. "And how do you explain Orville's interest? I think there's significance." He smiled at his niece. "Your sleuth sense is rubbing off on me, I fear."

"I've had the same feeling," she replied. She turned to Grover. "Just the fact that you were there with Hammie and Orville this weekend seems providential. In my experience, God is always working, but with a plan we can't always see. At first, anyway."

"Les thinks the clock's stopping was purely chance. He suspects Sam tried to start it again, and that's when the weight jumped the hanger, but the old man was too upset to stop and figure out what went wrong."

Hmmm. A mysteriously stopped clock: who wouldn't take it as a sign? And, at that moment, as Hammie pointed out, it had provided the framework Sam Miller needed to manage his grief.

"There's still the question of why the key was hidden in the clock in the first place," she reminded them. "It's obviously important enough that someone thought to hide it. But it certainly isn't an obvious spot to leave something for safekeeping."

"Unless the clock has mnemonic significance," Rocky reasoned. "I use mnemonic devices all the time for hiding valuables I use infrequently. Otherwise I'd never remember where I put them."

A fork dropped to the floor. Gracie turned, startled, as Grover stooped to pick it up.

When he went back to setting the table without comment, she said bravely, "I heard the rumors about Franklin and Patty. So unfair. . . ."

Grover paused, obviously weighing his next words. Then he spoke directly to Gracie. "My brother was a kind man, generous and gentlemanly to a fault. I don't know what you may have heard, but he was entirely honorable. He and Todd were the best of friends.

"He loved Patty as he would a sister. He responded to her needs with love, and was perhaps somewhat motivated by guilt — guilt because he knew Todd's shortcomings and couldn't persuade him to change. He was heartbroken by what happened, especially the way it all turned out in the end."

Gracie sighed. "That's the sense I got, hearing the story. Franklin found himself caught in a misunderstanding when he was trying to support Patty through a terrible time."

Rocky looked at his friend. "I know how much your brother meant to you. I didn't realize he was ever involved with the Millers."

Grover said gravely, "When you invited me this weekend, I knew it would be tough coming back. But I decided I needed to take the chance."

Grover looked gravely at Gracie. "Franklin never came back to Willow Grove. He talked about doing it when he was diagnosed with cancer, but it didn't happen." Grover exhaled. "You know what they say about hindsight. If we'd only known that was his last summer."

"I'm sorry," Gracie told him, her eyes tearing.

"I miss him. He was an architect and an avid conservationist, and he loved fishing. He even wrote several books on Illinois and Indiana streams. He had several commissions to design environmental education centers."

Grover smiled. "Even as he was dying, Franklin would encourage the rest of us. 'Each day that we live matters because of the effect we have on our world,' he'd say."

Rocky put his hand on his friend's

shoulder. "You obviously have every reason to be proud of him."

"He was my brother first, and for Franklin that was always the foremost thing. Connections were important to him. That's probably what got him in trouble with Patty. He only wanted to help his friend's wife."

The more Gracie heard, the more convinced she was that Marge was right. Franklin and Patty had been people injured by that deadliest weapon in the Devil's arsenal — gossip.

"Strange, things happening the way they did," Uncle Miltie said, bringing the conversation full circle. "You coming this weekend. You, Hammie and Orville coming together after all these years. Seems it was meant to be."

Yes, Gracie agreed.

"That's what hit me when I dropped the fork," Grover said. "I'd called Rocky about a case I was working on. He mentioned the trip, and I remembered my experiences fishing Acorn Lake."

"Then I told Hammie about Grover and he jumped at the chance to see him again," Rocky told her. "He demanded I bring him."

Grover nodded. "He seemed so excited to have me come, telling me Orville would be here too, as if it would be a reunion. But they were just boys when all of this happened, and I really never had known them.

"How strange it is for me to be reliving a scandal that involved my brother so long ago! I told you Franklin was upset and didn't want anything more to do with this place. But it wasn't the rumors about Patty and himself that were the problem. Everyone ignored them, for the most part. But when old Sam Miller insinuated that Patty and Franklin had been involved, that was what really hurt. Franklin admired Todd's father.

"And I haven't mentioned there was the matter of some missing Treasury bonds. Sam never came right out and accused her directly, but he made it clear he suspected Patty had taken them to protect herself and the boys in the event Todd ever left her. Then, when the Franklin rumors started, they fed his mistrust of her."

Grover glanced at Rocky. "That's the uncanny thing. When we found the key, and I thought about Cassidy, I remembered something Franklin had told me. My brother had mentioned once that Todd was thinking of leaving Patty and the kids, because he knew his father would always provide for them. Franklin never doubted Todd loved his wife. It wasn't that the marriage was bad — Todd's incurable wanderlust was the problem. Traveling gave him the freedom to do what he wanted, freedom not from Patty, but from his father. He just didn't want any part of that feed store."

Grover's expression softened. "Patty knew it, and so did Franklin. He became her advocate because he was her husband's best friend. The honesty between them helped her deal with the resentment she felt toward Todd."

Gracie glanced at Rocky, imagining what it would have been like if there had ever been some misunderstanding in their relationship. Rocky was one of her confidants. And he was special to her because he had shared a friendship with her husband. Her heart went out to the woman, Patty, whom she'd never even met.

"When you mentioned something valuable being hidden in the clock," Grover went on, "I thought of those missing Treasury bonds, the ones Sam suspected Patty of taking. They were Todd's — an inheritance from his grandparents. I don't know if they ever turned up or not.

"That's what struck me — it was like a kind of déjà vu, like I'd been through all this before."

Rocky glanced at Gracie. "Gosh, suppose those bonds are still in a box somewhere, after all these years!"

But did they have the right to probe a thirty-year-old wound simply to satisfy their curiosity? Gracie thought of Marge again, and the guilt she still bore for something that had spun beyond her control. She also thought of Orville and Hammie, and the rift between them. Could the bonds be what Orville was seeking?

Lord, what would You have us do?

She turned to Grover, thinking out loud. "Some things are not about chance. That key might hold the answer to a mystery whose time has come."

"I was thinking the same thing." Grover met her gaze. "I'm inclined to think Todd took those Treasury bonds and deposited them in a safe place. Cassidy may be that place."

Gracie would pray for wisdom.

In the meantime, a trip to Cassidy wouldn't hurt.

8

"I just got off the phone with Sherry Miller," Marge told Gracie. "The doctor says she has to take it easy for a while. Bed rest. But she says she feels fine. Her mother is there. She managed to get a flight up from Florida yesterday."

Gracie switched the receiver to the other ear. "I was planning to take them one of my cheeseburger loaves."

"I already volunteered us for more than one meal."

Gracie imagined her friend's grin. "I hope you're also volunteering to help me make them."

"Of course. I'm planning to include a lovely painted basket from the store for her nursery. Two better fairy godmothers this little baby-in-waiting couldn't ask for."

"Doing good is fun, but it's the most fun

when it's with a friend like you," Gracie declared contentedly.

"Well, I may be a somewhat clumsy kitchen aid, but I'm the one the good Lord gave you," Marge laughed.

"Thank heavens!" Gracie sent up a prayer reinforcing her words.

In fact, Marge Lawrence frequently was the wind behind Gracie's sails, encouraging her to step out and take the challenges that she might have sidestepped otherwise. It was Marge who'd dared her to "live dangerously" and return her hair color to a variation on the red shade with which she'd been born.

On the other end of the phone, Marge was now quiet. "By the way, I ran into Orville in the feed store this morning, when I stopped to pick up food for Charlotte. It felt strange, after we'd been talking about him and his family."

Gracie reached for her note pad. *Case of the Grandfather Clock*, she scribbled across the top of the page.

"Since Hammie's mother-in-law will be staying with them for a couple of weeks, Orville says he may head back to Pennsylvania early."

Gracie prayed that God might use what time was left to mend his relationship with his brother.

"I asked if he'd found what he was looking for, but he changed the subject. In fact, he began quizzing me a bit unexpectedly."

Gracie's curiosity was piqued.

"He knows somehow that I still see his Aunt Polly. He told me he was worried about whether she has sufficient funds to cover her extended care at Pleasant Haven. He asked me if I knew about any of her investments, or if I thought his grandfather had provided anything for her care."

That seemed more caring than calculated, and Gracie told Marge as much.

"Maybe. But there was something about his manner that struck a wrong note. I think he was pumping me. Really, Gracie, I wish you'd been there. You'd have known how to respond. I'm afraid I wasn't much help. Polly and I are old friends, and closer ones since I moved my mother to Pleasant Haven. But I haven't a clue about her finances."

Gracie shared with Marge what Grover had told them.

"I knew there was a rift between Sam and Patty! Polly hinted to me as much. Gracie, this is all too coincidental to be ignored. I need to go see Polly, and I think sooner rather than later."

"Maybe we could drop in on your mother, as well."

"Of course." Gracie knew Marge's mother's condition was deteriorating. "She has some good days, but sleeps a lot now. She may not recognize you, but she loves company."

Suddenly Marge got quiet for a moment. "Really, Gracie, I know God moves in mysterious ways, but I do think the mystery here is what He wants us to discover. I've been praying about my role in this. I'd love to be able to clear Patty's reputation, for once and for all. It would mean a lot to me," Marge said softly.

Gracie replied by saying she wasn't sure how much they could do. She would simply have to keep on praying. "I know God cares about our relationships. And that He answers prayers. Orville and Hammie coming to peace with one another would be an answer to at least one prayer."

"I'm not sure that's possible anymore," Marge reminded her. "Orville says he's leaving. It's going to have to be long-distance mending for those fences."

Marge was right, but distance was nothing to God.

Gracie hung up the phone, lost in her own thoughts. She glanced at the list she'd scribbled on the pad: clock, gossip, key, sad family.

Barb was putting out the bells for the preview performance at Sunday morning's worship service when Gracie stopped in at the church.

Barb confided to her, "I've been enjoying this quiet time. It's our gift to God, this music we offer. It probably sounds strange, but I pray for each of you when I put your music in your folders."

She smiled. "And just now, I was envisioning us ringing 'Ode to Joy' this Sunday. I'm imagining a sweet sound in His ear. Silly, isn't it?"

"It's not silly at all." Gracie patted her friend's arm. "I feel the same way when I help plant the church's garden."

Gracie also appreciated her choir director's loyalty to the classical sacred music. She knew that in modern, market-driven churches, the older music was often sacrificed to what was in vogue. Gracie enjoyed the new praise choruses, but it was the age-old hymns that lifted the congregation up and above the present. Those familiar strains kept them connected to a continuum of worship.

"You do such a wonderful job of choosing

just the right music."

Barb smiled. "If we could just convince Estelle of that!"

"She'll probably always be on her mission to refine us!"

Barb nodded, chuckling. "Every time I begin to think she's given up, she launches a new crusade. She's already got quite a song list picked out for our Sweet Adelines. I'm actually glad she's taken on this responsibility. It's one less for me, and it's nice, for a change, just to be a voice."

"She'll do a good job." One thing that could be said for Estelle was that she was diligent. Her musical selections were intelligent and often demanding.

Barb went on to share with Gracie the news that Pastor Paul was hoping the bell choir would attract new congregants and new musical contributions. "There are folks in the congregation who are more instrumentally talented than we might realize. Many of them can read music, but they just can't sing."

Gracie thought of her own son, who'd hated singing in the choir, but loved playing trumpet for the high school band. In those days, they seldom featured instrumentals in the worship service. She was thankful to Barb for the change, and to their progressive pastor. Gracie remembered when Pastor Paul had shanghaied a few reluctant teens to launch a praise band. It had made an enormous difference in the adolescents' participation at Eternal Hope and in their appreciation of their church.

Their young minister had a desire to serve the Lord that was infectious, spilling over into almost every facet of their community church life. "We certainly are fortunate to have such enthusiastic leadership at Eternal Hope."

"To be honest, Gracie, some of my own enthusiasm's been at a low ebb recently. Estelle gets on my nerves, but she knows her music. I'm considering asking her to become my assistant director."

Estelle seemed a candidate only heaven could love. But she would jump at the chance. It might be good for both of them. And the choir would get a crash course in patience.

"I'm really excited about this bell choir," Barb said, changing the subject. "I'm ashamed to admit that I was a backsliding Christian in college. But it was my experience with a bell choir that brought me back. I played with a local congregation, and with folks of all ages. That was how I returned to the fold."

It did often seem God's best gifts were human ones. Gracie had never known this story from Barb's life.

"Pray for this project," Barb said. "And ask for a little extra patience for me, while you're at it."

"My mother used to warn me about praying for patience." Gracie chuckled. "She'd say it can only be learned — through having to employ it."

"By the way, Gracie, everyone's thrilled with your uncle's inspiration about the fish fry. He and Les really seem to be putting their heart into it, and they have a crew drafted. I do think, though, that they could benefit from your expertise in catering. Les has got grand ideas for a menu, but not always practical ones for serving several hundred. I told him to talk to you."

"Well, however they plan to add loaves to their fishes, I'm delighted to provide encouragement from the sidelines."

Gracie stopped at Anderson's Meat Market on her way home. She loved the old-fashioned store, with its vintage enamel and glass refrigerator displays and old-fashioned scales. Herb Bower was ahead of her at the counter paying for his order.

"Police business?" she teased. Willow

Bend's chief law enforcement officer could be intimidating, but Gracie knew him as a fellow member of her congregation, a loyal family man and friend. "Marybeth okay?"

"Actually, she thinks she's coming down with something — both kids had the flu last week. So, I'm running a taxi service and picking up groceries."

Marybeth was one of their best choir members, a lovely soprano. Gracie expressed her sympathy, hoping she'd be feeling better by the next weekend.

"That's why she's taking it easy, nursing whatever it is before it gets any worse. She's really looking forward to the fundraiser, and making progress toward getting those bells."

Bill Anderson handed Herb his change. "Tyne's the same way. The twins have hardly talked of anything else!"

The two sisters Tish Ball and Tyne Anderson complemented each other in every respect, from the way they coordinated their outfits to the way they finished each other's sentences. Longtime choir stalwarts, they were the obvious choice to blend their voices in the duet number Estelle had chosen as part of the Adelines program.

"You've heard that Uncle Miltie and his cronies from Hammie's are heading this fundraiser?" Gracie asked Herb.

"Yeah, your uncle wanted me to help out in the kitchen. I told him that I'd be a better parking lot attendant, but Les had already roped Jim Thompson for that job."

She smiled. "I'm surprised you weren't a part of that fishing excursion, seeing how much of Hammie's coffee you consume."

"Just doing my duty keeping the rustlers at bay! Miller's Feed Store is such a great old-fashioned place I often feel as if I ought to be wearing a big tin star on my chest when I walk in there!"

"Yeah, Miller's really takes you back!" Bill Anderson laughed. "But then this place sort of fits in with it. We had a wedding to go to, or I'd have been at the lake in a shot!"

"Hammie was a real sport to set it all up. And it sounds like it was pretty exciting," Herb added. "I ran into the Old Man of the Sea. Rocky sure looked rough."

Gracie assured him the newspaper editor was healing nicely, and they filled Bill in on the debacle as he took her order.

He put the rump roast she chose on the scale. "Looks like you're having company."

"Truth is, I bought one of those cook-books specializing in creative leftovers. The shredded beef roll-up looks even better than the Yankee pot roast I have planned."

"It felt just like old times, Willses and Millers coming together," Bill went on. "Maybe something good can come from Orville's visit, after all. Is he helping with the fundraiser?"

Gracie hadn't thought to ask.

"Let's hope he's finally got his act together," Herb said.

Bill nodded. "Orville was pretty wild, all right. He and his buddies were always getting into trouble. My dad used to say he just needed a good kick in the pants. And, as strict as Sam Miller was, I'd be surprised if he didn't deliver one or two."

"Does make you wonder what he's doing back in town," Herb added. "Marybeth's mother told her he's been out to Pleasant Haven to visit his Aunt Polly, so that's at least a good sign."

Gracie decided not to comment.

9

Cordelia Fountain cornered Gracie in the kitchen at the Garden Club luncheon. "That ambrosia was scrumptious! I may have to beg you for the recipe! The ingredients were in heavenly — or should I say ambrosial? — harmony!"

Gracie knew that the best way to deal with compliments was to accept them graciously. Coming from Willow Bend's often imperious tourist home owner, they were compliments indeed. Her Victorian mansion, where she took paying guests, was the pride of her life.

"Simply scrumptious!" Cordelia repeated. "Oh, and I meant to ask you, have you gotten any further on that genealogical research I was urging you to do?"

Gracie gave a small unnoticeable sigh. It's not like she wasn't busy enough already. But

Cordelia, as president of the local historical society, had a different set of priorities.

She had made the mistake of mentioning to Cordelia one day that she'd heard stories of a Revolutionary drummer boy on her mother's father's side, and the older woman had been fascinated. But Gracie had neither the time nor the curiosity to scour old records and cemeteries for validation. However, she was trying to inspire herself to make an effort if only for little Elmo's sake.

"My grandson asked for help with his family tree. He wanted the information for his school project," Gracie told Cordelia. "I do have an old family Bible, and I inherited a file box full of genealogical research from a great aunt. I really should sort and record it."

"Gracie, my dear, remember, we owe it to posterity, and to ourselves! How can one know where one is headed if it is not known from whence one came?" Cordelia lifted her chin with the grace only a one-time belle could pull off. "The road didn't start with the present, my dear."

"I know you're right," Gracie assured her. "I've loved history all my life, and sharing family stories that go back in time just makes us all part of it. This way, kids see that what looks like dusty book stuff is really connected to them!"

"Genealogical research is something I take very seriously." Cordelia narrowed her gaze. "And, Gracie Parks, so should you. I'd love to help discover more about your family history."

"Well, I still have that family tree to fill out for my grandson."

"Fine." Cordelia straightened her shoulders. "We'll start tomorrow!"

Cordelia ignored the look of panic on Gracie's face. "Don't worry. We'll go slowly. My special interest is local families — that, and Indiana history in general, you know."

"Well, you've lived in Willow Bend all your life." This gave Gracie an idea. She decided to tell Cordelia about Sam Miller and the clock and ask her opinion. But the answer was a quite different one than she expected.

"I'm surprised Lester didn't mention that his father built that clock for Sam," said Cordelia. So was Gracie!

"Lester's father built that beautiful old clock in the cabin?"

Cordelia nodded. "He sold clocks in his shop in Avery, but he also built them in his spare time. Back then it wasn't a matter of batteries!"

Gracie shook her head. "I know!"

"Ralph Twomley was an avid duck hunter. He and Sam Miller had belonged to the same club, and they both loved their retrievers. Those were the days, Gracie. There's a place in my memory that's sweet with the scent of Papa's cherry-pipe smoke. I used to love to listen to him and his friends on the back porch swing, swapping stories. The smell of Papa's pipe smoke was always soothing, compared to those pungent cigars the other men smoked."

Cordelia sighed. "My father dearly loved the outdoors. In autumn, especially. It's the season that always makes me think most of him."

She paused, savoring her pleasant recollections. Gracie said nothing, instead remembering her own father's fondness for hiking the hills behind their home.

"That was a long time ago," Cordelia said, breaking the silence. "When people cherished the past and collected clocks as the beautiful heirlooms they are. You know Lester has several lovely ones in his home. He inherited them from his father."

"I never thought about it."

"He worked in the shop with his father all through school." The older woman sighed. "Alas, manual clocks lost their popularity, and there just weren't enough of them to keep a person in business. Ralph retired and then, not long after, he died."

Gracie knew she needed to talk to Lester again. It was indeed curious he'd never mentioned his father's connection to the Miller clock.

"Busy tomorrow morning?" Marge whispered when Gracie slipped in beside her at choir practice.

Gracie shot her friend a quizzical look.

"Us. The nursing home. Tomorrow morning. I called Pleasant Haven just to check for sure that it would be okay. Polly's mind drifts a bit, but, lucky for us, in the direction of the past. She's really pretty sharp, mentally. She's only confined to a wheelchair now because of her osteoporosis."

Gracie had made sure Marge knew that when they went out to visit Polly Miller, Gracie wanted to stop in and see her mother, as well. She reached over to squeeze her friend's hand.

Tears welled up in Marge's eyes. "Thanks, Gracie. Seeing Mom with you always makes it easier for me."

Irene Baxter had been a woman to be reckoned with. Marge's mother had been strong-willed and courageous, a feminist, really, without ever carrying any banners. She'd been an inspiration to family and friends. Gracie ached for her friend and the loss she was bearing.

But Alzheimer's was a terrible disease to suffer, for the meek and mild as well as for those as formidable as Irene, who'd lived alone in Florida for years.

"Polly will help make sense of these puzzles," Marge assured her. "You never knew her well, but you'll see how terrific she is."

Gracie couldn't stop worrying whether they were doing the right thing, dredging up the past on no more than a hunch that the key they'd found unlocked a box holding missing Treasury bonds.

"Of course, it can't hurt to talk to Polly. Besides, you know I love a mystery!"

"Sherlock Parks," Marge quipped, "and Marge Watson! So, how did the luncheon go with the ladies of the Garden Club?"

"There were no leftovers is all I can say."

"I told you," Marge laughed. "They may look delicate, those old biddies, but they have hearty appetites! But who am I kidding? They're many of them the same age as us! I wish I could have helped!"

Gracie understood. Marge had a shop to run, even if her best friend often doubled as assistant chef — a skill, Marge joked, that didn't come naturally.

"Cordelia was there, of course. With a bee in her bonnet about my researching my family history — which just happens to be one of her favorite occupations. Oh, and she also told me about Les's father. . . ."

Estelle Livett brought them abruptly back to choir practice by putting her finger to her lips, and shushing them with an expression of rebuke. Gracie smiled sweetly, accepting the reprimand, and Estelle couldn't help but smile back. *You and me, Lord, we'll just have to love her into submission. For Barb's sake, too.*

Barb now called for practice to begin.

"Well, Sherlock, I'll be on your doorstep at ten sharp tomorrow morning," whispered Marge.

It was the choir director's turn to shush them.

Gracie was in luck. By the time she'd finished sorting and filing the sheet music that Barb had asked her to get ready for Sunday's service, Lester was the only one left in the sanctuary.

"Well, your scars aren't quite as visible as Rocky's," Gracie said, joining him by the door. "I heard that it was more like pro wrestling than fishing!"

"Rocky took a beating, all right, but he

was a sport about it. He just adopted a permanent scowl rather than respond to any of our teasing!"

Gracie smiled. "As I said, it was great of you guys to take Uncle Miltie along. He's older than any of you, for one thing, and addicted to his awful jokes, for another."

"Gracie, we all love Uncle Miltie, you know that. We totally panicked when he conked out."

"Thank goodness he seems none the worse for his experience!"

"He's a tough old bird, all right."

Gracie knew Lester was being honest about her uncle. Retired himself, albeit at a much earlier age, he often shuttled Uncle Miltie to the senior center, to story hour at the library, and, of course, to Hammie's store. Lester had even built a special step stool to make it easier for her not-always-so-spry uncle to climb in and out of his pickup truck.

"You've been a good friend to him."

"Friendship is a two-way street, Gracie. Uncle Miltie is good company — and he really listens. That's a gift, and one that I, for one, am honored to accept."

She was touched. "El was fond of saying, 'You can bank on any friendship where interest is paid.' "

"Amen to that!" Lester turned to look more closely at her. "So, what do you need, Gracie?"

She felt a bit hesitant at first, but told him what she'd learned from Cordelia. "I confess I just can't stop puzzling over the clock and what it's trying to tell us. Your own connection to it was surprising, to say the least. Why didn't you mention it?"

He flicked the last switch and motioned toward the door. "I'll walk you to your car."

"Strange how the string from that key got caught in the works."

"Truth is often weirder than fiction. That's what makes for good mysteries, right?"

"I suppose, but it sure sets a person wondering."

"So, you've come to me to help satisfy your curiosity."

Gracie nodded. She didn't know what to expect.

"Well, just like Cordelia told you, my dad built the clock. Sam saw one we had in our house and wanted another exactly like it. It was to be a gift to his wife and an heirloom for the child they knew would be the only one they'd have. Florence was delicate, you see, she'd had several miscarriages, and she lived with diabetes all her life."

They now had stopped beside Fannie Mae. "Interestingly, Florence was an only child, and her parents were quite wealthy. They actually helped Sam establish the feed store. And they doted on Todd. So it seemed only natural they'd leave everything to him when they died."

Gracie looked at him. "Was it a lot?"

"I don't know, but the dad was a banker. Most of what he left them was in stocks and bonds. That's what I heard, anyway."

"So how do you think the key ended up in the works?"

"How would I know? Like I said, the truth can be pretty odd. I tend to think the clock stopped on its own, and the key got there sometime later."

He paused, with a troubled expression in his eyes. "The Millers have had more than their share of tragedy to endure over the years. Whatever I thought, I kept my opinion to myself."

She smiled at him, approving of his caution.

"I always wanted to be a watchmaker, to follow in my father's footsteps." He laughed. "We have a lot in common, Hammie and I. I knew my dad's business was failing. Folks weren't interested in getting their timepieces fixed anymore. They could buy a new clock cheaper than we could fix them. And franchised distributors could deliver mail-order seeds a lot cheaper than Hammie could.

"The days of the independent farmer were waning, almost in relation to the growth of consumers interested in cheap, replaceable products over quality service. Times were changing, as they say."

He lowered his gaze. "I'm a little ashamed I didn't take the risk and buy the business. I didn't mention my father built that clock simply because of old regrets. And you can't change the past — it doesn't take a watch-maker to know that. I admire Hammie for sticking to his guns, emphasizing service over price. He's proving that quality mat-ters, and personal relationships do, too."

Gracie stood there, impressed by the character of a man whose nature she'd long taken for granted.

Lester went on. "Hammie's a good man. And a forgiving one. That's probably why he's been so gracious to Orville, even after what he did."

Gracie looked at him, perplexed.

"I thought you knew this — Hammie in-herited the business, you see, but Orville be-lieved he still had a vested interest. This was after his grandfather had allowed Orville access to a pre-existing inheritance of his own. But the son-of-a-gun still insisted that his brother pay off his 'share' in the store. If old Sam Miller had known that, he'd have been rotating in his grave.

"It was tough for Hammie, coming up with the money after his grandfather died. All he had was the business, and what his brother wanted was a hefty piece of change. But Hammie did it, and never seemed to begrudge Orville a penny. But did he appreciate it? Not that I can tell. As far as I know, Orville never wrote or called. Now he's just turned up out of the blue, looking for something valuable of Sam's that he might have missed getting his share of before."

Lester shook his head. "That's what made that fishing trip so strange. Who would have thought that Orville, Hammie and Grover Wills would be in that cabin at the same time? It's got all the makings of a good mystery, all right, Gracie. I'll give you that."

"I've also been hearing something about the deaths of Hammie's parents," Gracie said cautiously.

Lester was watching her steadily. "So, what fed the rumors?" she asked. "Why didn't the police investigation put them to rest?"

"It was Patty's accident," he said after a

moment. "It threw the whole town for a loop. None of us could believe it, coming so soon after her husband's death. She and Franklin had been mighty friendly. People talk. And then Franklin never returned. It's funny how ghosts have a habit of revisiting the scene of the crime."

He looked at Gracie. "Finding that key was spooky. And you're not the only one asking questions, Gracie. Orville has quizzed me, too. He knew my dad made that clock."

"I thought he was interested in his grand-father's journals."

"Seems that key is taking precedent."

"What did Orville want to know?"

"That leads us back to pure speculation," Lester warned her. "I told him as much. He wanted information from me I couldn't give, like whether or not the string attached to the key could have stopped the clock. And whether or not I thought it had been in the clock since before his father's death.

"Frankly, Gracie I don't know. I don't know who put it there, or whether I even care. There are a lot of hard feelings and pain associated with that time. I don't care to revisit it. And that's another reason why I didn't come out right away with the fact that my father made the clock. I just have a hard time dealing with it all, that's all."

Gracie looked at him with sympathy.

"Why all the interest now? That's what I asked Orville."

"What did he say?"

Lester snorted. "Pretty much just what you'd expect from Orville Miller. He claimed everyone in town had a grudge against him, and that he was only looking for his due."

"His due?"

"A bigger share of the Miller money, what else? But Sam Miller, as I said, was more than fair, and then Hammie on top of that. Orville Miller wound up with more than a full measure of his grandfather's inheritance, whether he cares to admit it or not.

"Sam Miller was a fair man. He knew both of his grandsons. He knew Hammie would make a success of the business. And he'd be rip-roaring mad that Orville was back here, eager to stick his nose in the feed-bag again. Feed-bag — pretty apt, huh? Mark my words. Whatever Orville's after, it isn't forgiveness, or Hammie's friendship."

Gracie prayed he was wrong.

10

Polly Miller was in the solarium, sitting in her wheelchair, when Gracie and Marge arrived at Pleasant Haven. Her short-cropped white hair was still lustrous, and her bright blue eyes, set off by the pale pink rouge she wore, gave the elderly woman a youthful aspect.

Soon they were chatting about life in Willow Bend as it had been over the past decades. Gracie merely sat and savored the exchange. Polly was enjoying herself, obviously, remembering many colorful Willow Bend personalities and testing her memory against Marge's.

"Have you heard from Hammie?" Marge asked gently.

The old woman smiled. "I'm going to be a great-grandmother, in spirit if not in fact. Those boys are like my own grandsons."

"You're beloved by them, as well," Gracie reminded her.

"I remember when your husband was mayor," Polly told her. "He did a fine job. Sad, he died so tragically. Like my Todd . . . and Patty."

Gracie moved closer to take the old woman's cool hand. "There isn't a day that goes by that I don't miss him."

"Thank goodness for memories!" Polly smiled. "Sometimes I can't tell you what I had for breakfast, but I remember Todd's wedding day. And their calling me with the news they were expecting."

She smiled. "Thomas Samuel Miller. Todd Strobel Miller. Hamilton Thomas Miller. Orville Edward Miller — all my menfolk!

"I remember when Hammie lost his first tooth, and when Orville hit a home run in a strikeout season. I remember all those things. But then I can't recall what day it is for a whole week."

"Tuesday," Marge offered.

"Doesn't matter," Polly told her. "They're all the same to me." She chuckled.

"I always wished for a long life, but there's a certain sadness about outliving your contemporaries," Polly said. "Of course, I still have the children, but it's not the same." She paused for a few minutes while Gracie and Marge waited patiently.

"I thought I would be terribly lonely, but I'm not — just tired. Ready to go home, that's all. It was the worst after Sam died, he was the last in our family. God became my best companion. I don't know why I didn't seek Him out earlier. I guess I was too busy, like everybody else. But God was never too busy for me."

Gracie loved hearing her say this. It was exactly what she felt, too. Plus, she knew the right thing was to trust His heart, even when she could not see His hand.

"I was just chatting with the Lord earlier this morning," Polly told them. "He reminded me that you were coming. I get a little confused, but He's patient. All of a sudden I remembered a photograph I have of Patty and you, Marge."

She reached into her pocket to pull out a snapshot of a pair of adolescent girls. "I always meant to give this to you."

Gracie took it first and studied it. "You were pretty, Marge darling, just like now!"

"Beautiful! But neither Patty or Marge could take credit for their good looks then." Polly touched Marge's cheek. "Now, it's the soul's doing. You are beautiful, my dear. I can see that even with these old eyes."

Marge was touched. "I wish I could convince my reflection of that! I don't even clean the fog off the mirror anymore."

Polly laughed. "You still have a sense of humor."

"And you've actually gotten better eyesight!" Marge kissed Polly's forehead. "Thanks for the compliment. It's made my day."

"I can tell you one thing," Polly assured Gracie. "I remember the good people. I remember you and your husband. And Arlen. He was a fine student — and a sweet boy."

Gracie thanked her, and went on to tell Polly that Arlen was now married, with a son of his own, and living in New York City, where he worked as an editor. Polly then shared memories of other students, and the rest of the visit passed quickly.

"Well, you didn't come out here just to reminisce with an old lady." Polly patted Marge on the cheek again. "But I love you for it."

"Gracie says they found what looks like a key to a safe deposit box in the old clock out at the cabin," Marge said. "It might have been the reason it stopped."

"That clock stopped because its heart was broken. Now I'm glad it's gotten over it." Polly smiled. "Hammie told me what happened, and that he restarted the clock in the new baby's honor. That child is blessed before it's even born."

Gracie agreed.

"You know, Sherry might have lost that baby a few days ago, but she didn't. We were praying for her all that morning. Then I heard the clock was running again." Polly glanced at Gracie and Marge, her pale blue eyes glistening. "I reminded Hammie of that. He's been blessed.

"When the crisis has passed, it's so easy to forget who got you through it. It's too easy these days for young people to find a reason not to attend church. Sherry and Hammie are Christians, but they need a little nudge now and then to stay regular. Maybe that's why the Lord keeps me around." Polly laughed. "I'm here to get those two kids to church."

"They pick her up Sundays to take her," Marge explained to Gracie.

"I've been praying for those boys since before they were born," Polly now said. "I do realize that there's no time ever wasted in prayer, but I'm getting old. I sure wish God would set Orville on a better path."

Gracie smiled. "Maybe he already is. Hammie's such a splendid example."

"Orville came out to see me the other

day." Polly sighed. "I want to believe he's grown up, accepted some responsibility — but I'm just not sure. He wanted to know where Sam had kept Todd's legal papers — the will and such. Of course, he insisted he was only trying to set some things straight."

Gracie glanced at Marge. "You think he's going to make some new legal objection — after all these years?"

"Everything Todd had went to Patty, and then that was divided between the boys in a trust when she died. Everything. If he contests anything, it would be Sam's will. My brother was a shrewd businessman, and a wise judge of character. But he was fair with Orville, I won't argue about that. Myself, I'd never have given that boy as much as Sam did. Orville squandered his inheritance."

Gracie weighed her next words. "Someone said something about there being Treasury bonds from his other grandparents."

Polly leaned back in her wheelchair and laced her fingers, as if she, too, were weighing her words. "Sam thought Patty took them. I don't know, they were worth about forty thousand dollars. Personally, I figured Todd squandered the money. My nephew was never any good with money. And he liked what he called the 'good life.'

Sam knew that. But such bonds can't be traced. And I don't think he really wanted to know the truth."

"Sam didn't report it after Patty's death?" Marge asked.

Polly shook her head. "Todd was Sam and Florence's only child. And her parents were rich. As much as my brother hated to admit it, that boy was spoiled.

"I explained that to Orville. He thinks his grandfather hated him — it was just the opposite. He loved Orville because he was so much like Todd. I think that's why Sam didn't really discipline him. Orville took advantage of his grandfather because he sensed this."

Tears rimmed Polly's eyes. "It's Hammie I really felt sorry for. He's been loyal always, so much so he's gone unnoticed. My brother wasn't sentimental, so he never told those boys how much they meant to him. Sam called them a gift from God — a lifeline against grief's undertow. He said he never would have made it without them."

She looked at Gracie. "But why couldn't he tell them that?"

So many things were always left unsaid. Words could hurt, but they could also heal. "But you were able to right that wrong, if you explained all this to Orville. Maybe that will make the difference." Gracie waited for Polly's reply.

She nodded. "He's promised to visit me as often as he can while he's here. Perhaps that's another reason God keeps me around."

The older woman patted Gracie's hand. "That's not answering your question. See what I said about my mind — all over the place. Anyway, Sam was upset about the bonds. I knew he suspected Todd, but his grief caused him to accuse Patty. Franklin was there, and I think my brother was striking out, trying to blame someone for his loss. I think Patty knew Todd had taken them, but she didn't say. She had so loved my nephew in spite of all his shortcomings."

"And Franklin loved Patty for her loyalty to his friend," Marge said.

"Sam recognized that. He admitted as much to me later. But he didn't want to believe that his son had squandered all that money."

Gracie murmured under her breath, "Money — what it does to us."

"I felt terrible, too," Marge went on. "I played a part in causing her more grief."

Polly reached for Marge's hand. "I told you then, and I will tell you again. It was an accident. Patty wasn't driving recklessly, she went up there to be alone. She was upset about the rumors and the confrontation with her father-in-law. You know how unpredictable the weather can be in the winter? Marge, don't blame yourself."

Polly looked at Gracie, still holding Marge's hand. "Hammie's just like his mother," Polly told Gracie. "He goes off to cool down when he's mad. Patty was angry with Todd for dying. She was furious with her father-in-law. She was upset with the gossip, too, but she knew who her friends were. Marge, you weren't the only one to see her with Franklin."

Marge was quiet.

"Franklin stopped by the house quite often. It bothered Sam, too. I think it fed his suspicions of her. And maybe he was a little bit worried she might become interested in him. Patty was still young and attractive, and Franklin was a good man."

Polly grew quiet. "Secrets are so hard to keep. You take a risk when you share them with someone else, because then they risk turning into gossip. I've learned to take my secrets to God — then it becomes prayer. And that's the best we can do for anyone."

Indeed it was. Gracie liked this old woman, and only wished they'd become friends much earlier.

"Thank you for coming," Polly told them, a serene expression on her face.

They each embraced her, feeling incredibly blessed.

Gracie and Marge headed over to the Millers' house after leaving Polly. Hammie and Sherry had bought a post-World War II ranch on the edge of town, with a more than ample yard for Hammie to carve out a truck patch for his vegetables. He loved sharing produce with friends, and basked in compliments for what were known as the biggest and sweetest tomatoes in their corner of Mason County.

Hammie had also built a large, elaborate deck on the back of the house. Sherry grew perennials that spilled out of the beds and boxes. It made Gracie chuckle to think of them as a handsome, modern version of the Grant Wood painting of the stoic farm couple. Hammie Miller holding an upright pitchfork wasn't that far a stretch, except that his cheeks were rosy and not gaunt.

Ellen Croft met them at the door and invited them in for tea on the deck. Sherry was watering an ebullient clematis when she looked up to see Gracie and Marge walking toward her.

Marge hugged Sherry. "Aren't you supposed to be resting?"

"The doctor says fresh air is good for me." She glanced at Ellen. "And, rest assured, my mother won't let me do anything she thinks may jeopardize a healthy first grandchild!"

Gracie set her basket on the table. "Your meatloaf's ready to be warmed up. We included potato salad and some slices of spice cake."

Ellen took it all off to the kitchen. According to Sherry, who looked bright with health and happiness, everything was fine.

"That's wonderful. We're so relieved, aren't we, Gracie? But we knew you were getting the right care. I've loved Hammie since he was born, and I'm so excited he's starting his own family."

Sherry laughed. "I can feel cheerful now, but I *was* worried, that's for sure. That's why Mom's here, to spoil me a little."

"A lot," said Ellen, rejoining them.

Sherry now let a shadow cross her face. It seemed that the Miller brothers had exchanged angry words earlier that morning.

"Oh, Sherry," Gracie said, "I'm sorry this is something you have to be troubled by, now of all times."

Sherry sighed. "Orville didn't even say goodbye to anyone when he left the house. I was in the laundry with Mom and heard the door slam. I thought he'd come back, but when we checked, we saw his bag was gone, too."

"He was just so rude to Hammie!" Ellen added. "But, here, have some shortbread and lemonade." She had set a tray down on the table in front of them.

As she served them, Ellen explained that the argument actually had begun because of her. "That old key's now somehow missing, and Orville accused me of running it through the wash. But I always — always! — turn pockets inside out before I wash them, I told him. And I know I did that with the pants Hammie wore at the cabin."

"He didn't believe her," Sherry said. "He accused Hammie of hiding the key to keep him from those journals he's looking for."

Ellen added, "Of course, we're not even sure there are any journals. Orville's rummaged through about everything in the office, though so far he seems to have paid little attention to anything particular. And Hammie doesn't remember specific record books. He checked all the ledgers first — nothing. And Orville didn't seem interested in double-checking, despite claiming he's convinced Hammie lied."

Sherry eyed her mother. "Now, we

mustn't jump to conclusions."

"Orville always was the harder of the two to love," Marge admitted.

Ellen sighed. "I may be prejudiced, but I simply don't like him."

Sherry sighed. "Orville's accused Hammie of inviting Mom to visit simply to get rid of him. And that's just not true." She smiled at her mother. "She happened to come a little sooner, to make sure I was taking care of myself properly."

"It's too bad they've parted with such bad feelings. Hammie and Orville seemed to be getting along pretty well at the cabin," Gracie told them.

Sherry nodded. "Hammie is really trying. He wants a relationship with his brother. But Orville always seems so angry. About exactly what we're never sure. Over dinner they make small talk, but then something is said and the air chills. It's awkward for both of them, I understand. I try to get Hammie to talk to me about what's bothering him. . . ."

"Of course this continual tension must be awful!" sympathized Marge.

Sherry glanced at her mother. "It's just that my husband has done so much for his brother, and that the only time Hammie hears from Orville is when he needs money. But then it's always a guilt trip about how Sam preferred Hammie, and how my husband got everything, leaving Orville with nothing. But it is simply not true."

"He wasted his inheritance, you know," Ellen told them. "And however much it was, it would never have been enough — at least as far as Orville was concerned!"

"But it sounds like he's doing all right these days," Gracie told her. "He's bought a place in Pennsylvania and is hoping to do some farming."

Sherry's mother was unconvinced. "So he says."

Gracie now went over what she'd just heard. "Orville thinks you lost the key in the wash?"

"Or threw it away when I cleaned out his pockets. But I never saw it," Ellen said. "Hammie put those pants in the clothes hamper."

"He put his money clip, change and pocketknife in the dish on the counter," Sherry told her. "That's his habit. He thought he'd put the key there as well, but it's gone."

"So you assumed it went through the wash?" Marge said.

"I didn't assume anything!" Ellen was indignant. "I did the wash, and I checked the pockets. There was nothing in them. And I'm not in the habit of tossing things that don't belong to me into the trash!"

Sherry patted her mother's hand fondly. "My brother-in-law had no idea who he was going up against. This is a woman who means what she says and says what she means. If she says she turned out the pockets and there was nothing in them, then she did, and there wasn't!"

Gracie and Marge laughed.

"Hammie's really upset about his taking off like that," Sherry now said. "I called him when I noticed Orville's bag was gone. And he's left no note, telephone number or address."

Ellen pointed out, "You probably won't hear from him again until he wants something."

"But he didn't ask for anything this time, right?" Gracie was still trying to get things straight. "And we're not even sure he took the key."

Sherry thought for a second. "He spent a lot of time in Grandpa Miller's office. As far as I know, he didn't take anything. But Hammie would never check. He really wants to trust Orville again, Gracie."

Gracie rested her elbows on the table and,

lacing her fingers, set to thinking. *Lord, what are we to do?*

"You know," Sherry told them, "one of the things that attracted me to Hammie was his steadfast goodwill. He just refuses to believe that something or somebody is hopeless."

"Orville has brought this on himself," Ellen reminded her daughter. "He's the one who's taken advantage of your husband. You don't owe him your sympathy, honey. And fretting over this isn't good for your baby."

Gracie felt at a loss as to how to respond. Some children were just easier, it was true. But even the most difficult and mischievous ones needed acceptance — to know someone loved them even at their unloveliest.

Maybe love was the inheritance Orville was really seeking.

"Orville does seem to resent everything about Willow Bend — and us," Sherry was resigned. "And I don't know what we can do to change that. Maybe it's better for all of us that he's gone now." Sherry paused and seemed to reconsider.

"He is Hammie's brother." Sherry glanced to Gracie for support. "Pastor Paul was talking about us bearing with one another just last week. We're called to forgive even when the offender has not asked. It's the right thing to do."

Gracie agreed. Love was not about judgment but about acceptance. Whether or not Orville deserved it wasn't the issue at all. The Lord Gracie loved so well was eternally the God of the second chance.

11

"I don't know what you think you'll un-cover," Rocky said, pulling his little black car up in front of Lou's Diner in the little town of Cassidy. Gracie had no idea either. Knowing it was somehow part of the mystery, Gracie felt she had to see for herself.

However, what she found was none too encouraging. Cassidy was little more than a couple of convenience stores and a gas sta-tion. Its showpiece was a chrome-and-alu-minum diner. Lou's looked to be something a traveler might expect to find along Route 66, where a tourist would be attracted for nostalgia's sake. But in Cassidy, it was just part of the landscape and appeared to be the place the locals came for coffee and conver-sation.

"It's a lovely day for a drive, you have to admit," Gracie pointed out, trying to appeal to Rocky's better nature.

He thought for a second. "But am I driving on a lovely day for the sake of that lovely day, or am I squiring Nancy Drew around because she preferred to leave her own roadster at home?"

Gracie grinned and pointed toward the restaurant. "But this does seem to be your kind of restaurant, with hot and cold running ketchup. My treat, what do you say?"

He pulled the sun roof closed. "Let's hope the food is less depressing than its surroundings."

He unfolded himself with a little difficulty. Gracie was tempted to mention his expanding waistline, but decided it was a better moment for keeping her opinion to herself.

She knew Rocky was just humoring her request to visit Cassidy. She also realized that back at the office of the *Mason County Gazette* he was experiencing an end-of-the-week crunch. Yet her friend had agreed to this excursion, and she loved him for it.

"Suppose someone here remembers Todd? Or can throw some light on what that key opens?"

Rocky snorted. "There isn't a bank to be seen. Even if anybody remembers Todd Miller, it's been thirty years. Gracie Parks, admit it, this is a goose chase of the wildest sort."

He was probably right.

She sighed.

Rocky softened. "Well, okay, it was a nice drive. And I trust your hunches, really I do. And I suppose I needed a day away from the job. With my favorite sleuth."

She appreciated the effort he was making. She couldn't help but feel better.

"Indiana sure is pretty. Especially this time of year." Rocky opened the door for her. "Didn't Grover say they have good fishing in these parts?"

"Perfect conversation starter."

They chose to sit at the counter, sharing it with an old-timer and a waitress in a gaudy pink matching smock and pants. Her makeup was bright but so were her sparkling violet eyes. She had a friendly smile.

"Shirley," her nametag read. Gracie decided right away she liked her.

"Looks like someone tripped big time," Shirley joked as she studied Rocky's still bruised face. "So what did the other guy look like?"

Rocky studied the menu. "Fishing accident," he responded, none too convincingly.

Shirley reassured him, "I like a man who

can hold his own in a fight — even with a fish." She winked.

The old man laughed, and Rocky tightened his lips.

"You got any coconut cream pie left?" he asked.

"Man after my own heart," Shirley pronounced. "Life is too short, so you might as well start with dessert."

Gracie ordered a cup of the chicken noodle soup she smelled simmering in the kitchen. Rocky decided on a hot roast beef sandwich — claimed by Shirley to be the specialty of the house — with gravy on his fries and a side of slaw. He also reserved a slice of the coconut cream pie.

"I hear there's good fishing around here," Rocky said, accepting a cup of inky black coffee.

The old man swiveled to face Rocky. "Blair Mills is best this time of year — a couple miles out of town. The mill is long gone, but the creeks seem to breed the biggest, fattest trout you've ever seen. We get people from all over the place fishing our streams now."

"Nice town," Gracie pointed out.

He shook his head. "Not any more."

"Nothing left in these parts. It used to be a farming community," Shirley said, sliding a glass of iced tea in front of Gracie. "But that's in the past. They're all corporate farms now."

"Where you all from?" their fellow diner wanted to know.

Gracie told them. They both knew people in Willow Bend, and Gracie's beautician turned out to be Shirley's ex-husband's niece by marriage. Gracie brought up the name Todd Miller as casually as she could manage.

"I remember him vaguely," the man said. "Ran a display over at the county fair every summer. Liked to fish — he and his friend came here a lot. I think he might have had something to do with that fish hatchery outside of town."

"Before my time," Shirley claimed. "I just happen to be a lot younger than I look."

"Well, you look like a prune to me, so I guess that makes you a raisin," her regular quipped. I'll have to remember that one for Uncle Miltie, Gracie thought to herself.

Then their new friend suddenly remembered something else. "You know, I think that guy used to rent a place out on the creek. He got to be friends with Fred Spring — some kind of business venture. Like I said, I think it had something to do with the preserve out at the Mills."

Shirley snapped her fingers. "Hey, I do remember an equipment salesman who liked to fish! He came in here mornings for the breakfast special. He had a wallet full of pictures — pretty wife and kids."

Gracie told her about the key they'd found.

"Well, there's no bank in town anymore. They moved to Farmington, like almost everything else. That was about ten years ago." Shirley topped Rocky's cup. "Cassidy isn't much — just the few houses you saw along the highway. Everybody goes into Farmington for what they need."

"Got pretty good fishing still, though!" The old-timer smiled. "We may have lost the agricultural edge to the corporations, but folks still come here summers to enjoy the lakes and streams. We even got that experimental hatchery I just mentioned, outside of town."

"There's only a few diehards like Vince and me left," Shirley told them. "You got to be independently wealthy, or else crazy, to stay here. Farmland as far as the eye can see, but the farmers are gone. No industry to speak of."

Gracie nodded in sympathy. The farming community around Willow Bend was starting to experience the same plight. Not-so-distant suburbs had begun to let their breath be felt on the countryside, even if the horrors of massive development schemes so far hadn't changed the landscape Gracie knew so well and cherished.

"Tell you what I do remember," Shirley said, pausing to ponder the significance. "The bank ran an ad right before it closed shop, saying it was merging with one in Farmington. The ad stated that unclaimed accounts would be transferred to some state holding fund. I was wishing I had a claim to some of that money. It was a long list, if I re-member correctly."

Gracie shot Rocky an I-told-you-this-would-pay-off smirk. "Do you remember the name of the bank?"

"Cassidy Savings and Loan, only one in town," Vince told her.

It is a safe deposit key!

The trip home was leisurely. Rocky, re-plete with roast beef and pie, was amenable to stopping at several roadside stands, where Gracie picked up a melon, some brown eggs and a jar of homemade corn relish. At the last minute, she added a couple of zucchini, for good measure.

"My mother used to make a zucchini dish with eggs and cheese that was pretty tasty," Rocky told her innocently.

"Is that a boast or a hint or both?"

He grinned. "Take your pick."

"How about a deal? You find out how banks or government agencies handle unclaimed property or inactive accounts, and I'll make you your mother's recipe."

"I could do that, if I didn't have a paper to get out. And this afternoon jaunt across the county with you, my dear, as lovely as it has been, does not produce the necessary copy to fill those empty column inches!"

He glanced her way. "You might try calling that pretty niece of yours. She's a lawyer, and would have easy access to a lot of those records. Besides, you wanted her to take a few days off. Maybe you could seduce *her* with one of your culinary bribes."

"And Carter does have a lovely voice," Gracie told him.

"What's that got to do with anything?"

An idea was crystallizing. "Barb wants to do a Sweet Adeline piece for your fish fry. Carter sang in one in college, I remember. Maybe I could get her to join us. That would be a nice treat for her. And, she could show me how to follow up on unclaimed bank storage."

Then she stopped to consider for a moment.

"But I know that if I ask Carter to check

this out for me, it would simply become one more boulder in the mountain of work weighing her down. Her office is already notorious for that. And knowing her boss's reputation, what she needs is a respite not a surfeit. She works too hard — just like her father."

Gracie's beloved brother, Carter's dad, had died of cancer when he was far too young. A flash of sadness reminded her that she, like Polly Miller, now was the matriarch of her family. It was her responsibility to hold every one of them up in prayer, and to keep them in her heart at all times. Yes, she would call Carter as soon as she got home.

"That would be the State Attorney General's Office," Carter informed her over the phone.

Carter went on to explain that Illinois had something similar, as did most of the states: The Department of Unclaimed Property.

Under a law passed by the Indiana General Assembly, money or property left unclaimed for a certain amount of time would be returned to the state after it had been left with a "holder" such as a bank, insurance company or other business organization. Carter thought the state had to hold on to it for twenty-five years.

Gracie scribbled notes on her pad. Money and property ended up in the state account when the holding institution had no way of contacting the owner, when he had left no forwarding address, or when his family neglected to notify the institution of his death. The Attorney General's office usually set up a booth at the Indiana State Fair to help people understand this law and to look into unclaimed accounts.

"Is that the only way to check a name?"

"They've got a computer-generated database. Anyone can search for a match. You can access it through the state government web pages." Carter was intrigued by her aunt's story of the clock and the key and the vanished Cassidy bank.

"By the way, Aunt Gracie, I hope you have a checklist of your own financial assets, and that everything is in a place where it can be easily found. I know we did update your will, but that was years back. I was just a law clerk then."

Gracie understood her niece's concern and was grateful for her attentiveness. They both realized the work had been done right after El died, at which time Gracie had also created a living will. "I really should update both documents," she acknowledged.

Then she remembered Carter's need for

a little well-deserved rest and some extra mothering. "Have you given any more thought to celebrating your birthday with me, dear? We could look at my papers then."

"I'll bring my laptop, and we'll look up your names, too."

"You mean you *can* come?" Gracie's heart skipped a beat.

"I was going to phone you tonight. This morning, my boss called me into his office to congratulate me on the case we'd just won. I did a lot of the legwork. Anyway, he told me to take a few days off — a birthday present, he called it. Can you believe it?"

Gracie just smiled. She'd expected nothing else.

"Aunt Gracie, I'm reading your mind: You're right, life does go better with prayer."

"Oh, my dear, that you understand is all I can ask!"

"You're coming up against a lot of strange connections," Carter said just as they were about to hang up. "Life sure is mysterious, isn't it?"

Yes, God kept life mysterious, that was evident enough. Yet, as Gracie well understood, that never meant a person should stop trying to figure it out. And she didn't intend to.

Gracie drew a deep breath. The apple-and-cinnamon scented air advertised her friend Abe's deli better than the breakfast-special poster in his window. Rocky usually took his morning break with Abe, and since she was en route to meet Cordelia at the library, she decided to stop there on the way.

She could enjoy an apricot danish while she updated Rocky on what she'd learned from Carter. Besides, Abe Wasserman was one of her favorite people anywhere — in Willow Bend or beyond.

Rocky was already seated at the counter, a book open in front of him. She perched herself on the stool next to his.

There was nothing like Abe Wasserman's apple strudel, except maybe his potato kugel, or cheesecake, or perhaps his mother's chicken noodle soup. They could not compete, of course, with her own mother's recipe for apple pie, but, then, they didn't try to.

Abe appeared, brandishing a coffee pot. "What can I get you, Gracie? The special's $4.95, but the advice is free."

"I'm just going to have cup of coffee, and maybe an itsy-bitsy piece of that apple strudel I sniffed coming in. I thought I wanted a danish but the cinnamon-sugar smell has made me powerless to order anything else."

He threw up his free hand after depositing the mug in front of her. "Your friend Mr. Gravino here is being his usual stubborn self!

"He thinks he knows baseball, Gracie! Just because he's hocked frankfurters at Wrigley Field doesn't make him an expert."

Rocky straightened his shoulders and leaned forward defiantly. "I grew up with Veterans Stadium practically in my back yard, and the Yankees were just a stone's throw away!"

Abe puffed himself up, and the men went into what appeared to be round two of their argument about an important trade. Gracie noticed Rocky's scrapes and bruises were healing nicely, in spite of his rejection of her nursing skills. She smiled, feeling blessed for having such a strong and caring advocate. Actually, she had two of them, although at the moment they were behaving like little boys.

Gracie made a time-out gesture. "I do need some advice, Abe, dear."

He grinned at her happily.

"My grandson needs me to detail his

family tree, and sketching it out for him made me think of the beautiful illustrated genealogy chart I saw on your wall. I thought, if I'm going to go to all that trouble, maybe I could get something like that for Arlen and Wendy for Christmas."

Abe smiled. "What you saw is my parents' wedding certificate. It's not really the same thing even though it does record pertinent dates. And it is beautiful — a lovely memento given to them by their congregation when they married."

"I remembered the names and the dates, and all the fancy lettering and scrollwork. I guess I thought it was a family tree of some sort."

He wiped his hands on his apron. "I have a catalog of Judaica somewhere here. You can probably order something like that. After all, the Jews wrote the book on genealogy. We've got families going back millennia. That's how they determined the priestly line."

"All the way to Jesus," she reminded him.

"Now, there was a Jew with a pedigree!" Abe laughed.

"Why the sudden interest in genealogy?" Abe wanted to know. She explained that little Elmo's project was the impetus. "Cordelia is going to tutor me at the library later today. She even knows how to access the files at the Mormon Temple in Salt Lake City — on the computer!"

"Well, there's proof positive you can teach an oldster a new trick or two." Abe crossed his arms, feeling satisfied. "Ask her if she would take on another pupil. I've always wanted to make some sense out of the hodgepodge I've collected over the years."

Rocky was watching the two of them with affection.

"We aren't getting any younger, Gravino. Who's going to remember any of this if we don't leave some of it written down for posterity?"

"Speaking of remembering for posterity!" Gracie turned to face Rocky. "Marge says that Polly Miller is going to be ninety soon. Why don't you do a feature story on her? She's given so much to this community, and she's delightful to chat with."

"Which you just happened to discover while tracking a lead on that old key," Rocky said. "I wonder that Uncle Miltie doesn't starve when you've got a mystery to unravel."

Abe looked perplexed, until she explained to him about the grandfather clock and the still unidentified key.

"It could belong to a locker of some sort,"

Abe pointed out. "Like one of those you rent at the bus station, or the post office. I used to keep a locker when I was a traveling salesman. I had a key like you describe."

Rocky stopped in mid-sip. "I didn't know you were in sales."

"Deli items for a meat packager in Chicago. That was way back in the days when I had hair." He slid his hand over his bald spot. "I was a looker back then, let me tell you!" Abe winked at Gracie. "I could sweet-talk the girls behind the counter into getting their bosses to order our full line."

"You can still sweet-talk the ladies," she told him.

Rocky put down the mug. "Really, Abe, I'm beginning to think you're on to something here. What if someone in the family, our traveling salesman, for example, picks up something of value that he can't take home. One of those lockers would be the perfect place to hide it. Then, say, he dies in an accident."

"Nobody would know he had it," Abe finished.

Rocky nodded. "Or, suppose he had an inheritance and was thinking about divorce. He might stash a bundle of Treasury bonds in a box to protect himself."

Something clicked in Gracie's mind. "Or,

maybe, the man had spending problems, and was forced to take the bonds to cover his losses. He could have been planning to report them as stolen."

Rocky exclaimed, "But then he died first!"

Abe threw up his hands. "Who and where is this guy?"

Gracie looked meaningfully at Rocky. She wanted him to see she was reluctant to accuse Todd Miller . . . even posthumously. Gossip was gossip, even if the object of it was no longer around to be hurt by it. After all, Todd had living relations, some of whom Gracie cared about a great deal.

"Buried," Rocky said. "And that's probably where his skeleton should stay, unless something significant requires our rattling his bones."

"Like the key turning up missing?"

It finally clicked for Rocky. "And Orville hightailing out of town the same day?"

"Orville Miller! Now, that's a family with skeletons. I remember the gossip." Abe shook his head. "You know what they say, a gossip is the devil's postman. His deliveries hit about every house in town. Nearly broke that sweet woman's heart."

"Patty?"

"She used to come in here. Sometimes

we'd sit and talk. Folks — they just seem to trust me, I guess."

Abe looked at Gracie. "Patty was struggling with a difficult marriage, and two little boys. Her father-in-law was putting pressure on her to get her husband to quit his job and come back to work at the feed store."

"But Todd enjoyed what he was doing. He was a personable fellow. I liked him, actually. Selling came easy to him, and it gave him the opportunity to travel."

Rocky stroked his chin, thinking out loud. "What we have here is a thirty-year-old treasure, possibly left in a locker or a bank deposit box. Orville turns up in town, supposedly looking for old journals. A key with 'Cassidy' scribbled on the back turns up in a grandfather clock that hasn't ticked for all those years. Now, that key is missing."

It occurred to Gracie that Grover would be returning at the end of the week for the fish fry. She'd be interested to hear what he thought about their discoveries.

"Why don't I plan something while Grover is staying with you?" Gracie suggested. "I could fix your zucchini casserole, and we could have a little party of sorts. I'll invite Marge. Oh, and did I say, Carter's going to be staying at my house — every time I talked to her recently, she seemed totally exhausted. So I talked her into coming for some R and R."

"I'll bring the dessert." Abe grinned. "It'll be great to see Carter again."

Gracie smiled happily. "Well, in fact, it's going to be her birthday celebration! Carter's turning thirty this weekend!"

12

Cordelia was in the reserved computer cubicle before Gracie arrived, already scrolling down through a list of names. "I have some Stephenses in my line," she announced without turning around, as Gracie came up behind her.

"How did you know my maiden name?" Gracie took the chair next to hers.

Cordelia smiled. "Your brother's daughter. That lovely niece of yours. She was out walking one day while she was visiting you last summer. She complimented me on my geraniums, and we got to talking. I have a pretty good memory for last names, especially when they cross my family lines."

Cordelia turned her attention back to the screen. "We've got some Massachusetts Stephens here, and a few from New Jersey. Might one of these families be yours, dear?"

Gracie got out the notebook in which she had copied the information from her mother's Bible. Cordelia scanned the pages. "My, my, Gracie, dear! It looks like you've got a lifetime adventure at your fingertips!"

They spent the next hour organizing data and backtracking family names from Gracie's great grandfather down. It didn't take long for Gracie to realize looking up one's ancestors could be almost as thrilling as unraveling mysteries. Meanwhile, Cordelia, entirely in her element, was only too happy to act as Gracie's guide to the intricacies of the research and its shortcuts.

"Sam Miller originally came from Pennsylvania," Cordelia told her. "His family were poor farmers. He gambled his way home across the Atlantic after World War II and used his winnings to buy the piece of land where he built the cabin. He cut quite a figure in those days.

"Florence was a Strobel — they were a rich Chicago family. She was spending the summer in Virginia with relatives when she met a handsome sailor waiting to ship out to war. Sam swept her off her feet, and they were married before his ship left for England."

Cordelia smiled. "So romantic! They ended up in Willow Bend because she wanted to be near her parents, and he wanted to live in the country."

"How did Polly wind up here?"

Cordelia clicked the mouse to print. "It's always good to keep hard copies, my dear. Remember to get yourself a proper binder, and some archival plastic sleeves."

Then turning back to Gracie, she continued. "Where was I? Well, Sam went off to war, and Florence returned to Chicago, expecting their first child."

"In those days, teachers would have to give up their jobs to marry. Polly had put herself through college, and she wasn't about to give up the career she loved. She never married, and instead cared for her invalid mother. Polly came out after her sister-in-law died, to help Sam raise Hammie and Orville."

Gracie glanced at her watch. "Oh, my! I've got bell choir rehearsal in an hour!"

"I love choir bells."

Gracie explained that they had a set on loan, and that they were going to use them in concert to kick off their fundraising campaign. She invited Cordelia to the fish fry.

"If you need another soprano for your Adelines?" Cordelia hinted, "I did have voice lessons. But I guess it's short notice."

Gracie smiled, knowing that here was

someone who could give Estelle Livett a run for her money.

Lester ran into Gracie as she was leaving the church office. She'd been helping with the filing there as she often did. "How's the mystery unfolding? Any leads on the key?"

She wished she had something to tell him, but what she'd managed to unravel seemed strands of different colors. How they fit together, she wasn't sure.

She felt it was still not right to share what she'd learned about Todd and the Treasury bonds. But she decided to ask Lester if he'd ever seen the unclaimed property booth at the state fair.

Lester thought a moment. "Nope, never noticed it. But didn't Orville say he went to the Pennsylvania State Fair shortly before coming out here? Didn't he tell us that's where he got the idea to experiment with grain seed?"

Yes, she did remember!

Pat Allen, the church secretary, now came out to join them. "I heard they've sold almost a hundred tickets to the fish fry. Word's out that you've been doing a great job organizing it!"

"I managed to get a terrific price on fillets from a wholesaler — since our catch slipped the bucket." He winked at Gracie, who couldn't help giggling.

Rocky and Uncle Miltie were in front of the television that evening after dinner. Soon her dear uncle was snoring softly in his padded recliner. Gracie waved Rocky into the kitchen, so he turned off the war movie and joined her.

Marge now appeared at the back door, carrying her little Shih Tzu. "Charlotte gets lonely cooped up in the house all day."

She put the dog down, shooing her over to play with Gooseberry, who was stretched out on the floor. The big orange cat managed a bored yawn, then ambled out of the kitchen. Charlotte tagged behind.

As she scooped out ice cream for the three of them, she shared what she'd learned from Carter.

"So, you think Orville got the idea about the accounts when he was at the Pennsylvania State Fair?"

It was a possibility. "We'll understand this better when we have Carter here with more answers to our questions." She put a plate of snickerdoodles in front of them.

"I actually tried to do a little checking on Orville Miller myself," Rocky now admitted. "All I know is that his last address was a post office box in Harrisburg, Pennsylvania. But beyond that I could learn nothing."

Rocky took a moment to swallow a large spoonful of rum raisin. "I asked Grover to see what he could dig up on the man. Unofficially, of course. On the first run-through, we've found out that he's defaulted on a couple of loans. He also disappeared with no forwarding address. The way I figure it, five years are unaccounted for. That's not saying Hammie didn't have some idea where he was. But it wasn't something any of us ever would have thought to talk about with him."

"That's right. But it seems pretty clear he's greedy — and not fussy about taking more than his share," Marge paused, for dramatic effect. "And now, he's got the key to the safe deposit box, and all those untraceable Treasury bonds in it!"

Gracie felt it necessary to defend Orville. "We don't know any of that for sure. The key is missing, but we don't know for a fact that he took it."

Rocky followed her lead. "And we don't even know for a fact what the key opens. Or that there's any money to be found. All of this is just speculation."

"But Orville's looking for *something,*"

Marge reminded them.

"My guess is that he's just always after cash for one reason or another. For some people, what they have is never enough and they can't hold on to it, anyway."

He leaned back in his chair. "All I can say is let's hope he's not found another way to cheat Hammie out of another chunk of his inheritance."

Gracie now said, "You know, I'm glad we have a system of innocent-til-proven-guilty. I hate to think the worst of anyone without all of the facts. And, even then, I don't like it!"

"That's the thing, Gracie. Once a reputation is broken, it can be repaired, but folks are going to keep an eye on the crack. And it doesn't look like Orville's even been trying to change the way anyone around here thinks of him."

She sighed sadly. "You're right."

"On a cheerier note," Rocky announced, "all the arrangements for the fish fry have been falling into place. Shows you that we guys can do this kind of thing quite nicely, thank you, if we put our minds to it."

He scraped the last streaks of ice cream from his dish. "Rum raisin for me. But what about Uncle Miltie? He began to snore pretty fast, but I'm sure he's dreaming of dessert."

"I have his favorite — peanut butter ripple — right here, and in a few minutes I'm going to wave it under his nose. That'll do the trick!"

"George Morgan is one lucky fellow. Gracie, you have made his golden years diamond-encrusted, I tell you. Who doesn't dream of that bottomless bowl of ice cream!"

"I'm lucky to have him," Gracie said simply.

"If anything was going to get me back into church, it would be your devotion, Gracie. I saw it when El died, and I see it in everything you do. Your serene conviction that God is in control almost convinces me."

Gracie looked at Marge, recalling their visit with Polly Miller. "A dear old woman reminded me of something I've known all along: Losses leave gaping wounds, empty spaces only God can fill."

"There's a lot of emptiness in the world, Gracie," Rocky said softly, meeting her gaze.

She nodded. "He's a big God."

13

After depositing her bag in her room, Carter bounded down the stairs, hit the living-room floor, and took a big whiff of the air wafting from the kitchen. "Oh, how I missed this place! And the intoxicating scent of chocolate-chip cookies baking!"

"Two whole batches!" Gracie informed her, enjoying her niece's pleasure.

"Where's Uncle Miltie?"

"Singing lessons," Gracie explained with a grin. "It seems a group of the guys who hang out at Miller's Feed Store decided to learn barbershop. Believe it or not, Rocky's giving it a try, too."

"The weekend's starting to sound like quite an extravaganza."

Gracie laughed. "As our Sweet Adelines expanded to include more members, more men decided to join the 'quartet.' I don't know what you'd call it now — but 'motley crew' probably describes it best!"

"Am I going to get to hear you all play those famous choir bells, as well?"

"A bunch of us are just trying to master a simple piece," Gracie told her, "and we're discovering it's no easy feat to get eight people to ring in time. Barb was a saint to take this on. But we're having a good time, and, for now, that's what counts."

Carter grinned, hugging herself, just like the little girl Gracie remembered. "I'm so glad you talked me into coming!"

"Do you want milk with your cookies? Or would you rather have coffee? I don't still think of you as a little girl, but milk's such a perfect fit with cookies that even many of us old folks prefer it!"

"Milk would be wonderful!" Carter reached for her computer bag where she'd left it on the couch. "Let's check out that information you asked for."

She set up her laptop on the table, and Gooseberry leapt up to investigate. His wide green eyes stared at the screen.

"Uncle Miltie's lent his computer to the Searfosses for a bit. Gooseberry must miss it — after all, the television doesn't have a keyboard for him to treat as a trampoline. But Joe wanted to become more proficient, and Uncle Miltie is just so generous. Besides, I think he worried that he was becoming a little addicted to the Internet!"

"You mean, he's never worried about his addiction to football games or home-improvement shows?"

Gracie laughed, as she watched Carter click her way through documents. "These are unclaimed property files?"

"*Mmm-hmm.* Miller is a common name. Almost all of the states have an unclaimed property division, but I started with Indiana. We've got all kinds of stuff here. Everything from unpaid wages to estate proceeds."

She stopped at "Todd Miller."

"I have four Todds here, but none are for safe deposit box contents. And none are for an amount large enough to interest our suspect."

"What about Patty Miller?"

Carter shook her head. "Maybe under a maiden name, or an alias. I checked every combination I could think of, and found no listing of unclaimed Treasury bonds. I did find something under Cassidy, but not in the unclaimed property."

Carter zipped through a few more files. "It's a patent for some type of pump for a fish hatchery. Willspring, with a T. S. Miller as one of the owners, sold it to a larger company specializing in aerators in 1986."

Gracie was perplexed. "That was almost ten years after Todd died. And what does it have to do with the key?"

"There's a register for Willspring in the unclaimed property files. It lists stocks."

"But what does that have to do with the key?"

"Perhaps nothing. Maybe the key's a red herring. But it could unlock the box that holds the stocks. T. S. Miller received over one hundred thousand dollars for that patent, and stock options, too. But what's actually in the box, if one exists? There's no way to access that information. I'm no magician."

Gracie leaned forward to read the screen. "So, what you're telling me is that there are no bonds for our Millers, but there are stocks. That doesn't fit with anything I've learned so far."

"A lot of small companies make limited stock, or a piece of the company, available to investors. That's how they grow. It's called venture capital. In this case, a small company owned the patent for a very lucrative invention. I didn't have time to do the research, but my guess is that the technology was innovative."

Gracie sat back in her seat, realizing that some of this information involved things she'd learned about before. "So, if this company was bought out by a larger company, are the stocks worth anything?"

"It could be a lot, but we simply don't know what kind of deal was made."

Carter took another cookie from the plate. "Have I eaten the entire batch? *Mmmm!*"

"What do you make of it?" Gracie asked.

"I just learned about the patent files," Carter sipped her warm milk. "I showed the Willspring one to the guy in our office who does that kind of corporate work, and he says that the stocks could well be unclaimed wealth.

"But like I told you, I haven't had time to follow up on this. I had a lot of work to wrap up before driving here." Carter smiled at her aunt. "If you're interested, I could check further when I get back. The company that bought Willspring has its home office in Chicago, which means I could even do it in person."

Carter was dressed to go jogging when Gracie, dressed in a new navy sweatshirt and pants, came down Saturday morning. "You look great, Aunt Gracie."

175

"I know we go at different speeds," Gracie said, "but I thought we could start out together, at least."

"That was my plan, too," Carter assured her. "With Gooseberry that'll be three of us."

"I intend to fix you a nice breakfast when we get back. Waffles with blueberry syrup."

"You're the best, Aunt Gracie! Now let's go work up an appetite!"

At the corner, they stopped to watch Gooseberry stalking something unseen under a rhododendron.

Usually, Gooseberry would follow Gracie for a while, until he got distracted or bored — then he'd turn tail and head home or to one his favorite haunts. That morning, he was keeping his two humans in eyesight.

"This is so pleasant, Aunt Gracie," Carter said. "Maybe I'll just walk this morning, and keep you and Gooseberry company."

At that moment Don Delano pulled up to the curb. "Gracie — and Carter! What are you doing in town? Not that there has to be a reason — it's just great to see you!"

"Hi, Don!" Gracie noted that she looked genuinely happy to see him, too.

"How long are you here for?" he wanted to know.

Carter seemed the most relaxed Gracie

had seen her so far. Maybe Marge was right, and she just needed a little romance.

Don announced, "I'm sure you know about the fish fry — maybe I could pick you up?"

"Do you believe I'm performing?" She smiled at him. "My aunt recruited me for her Sweet Adelines."

"Just keep my offer in mind!"

"I will." Carter's glance was sweetly flirtatious.

Gracie eyed her niece as Don drove off. "Should I ask?"

Carter sighed. "The problem is, I never seem to like the nice ones enough. Maybe I don't really want to meet Mr. Right."

Gracie considered this. "You have a high-powered career."

"You know I've always dreamed of having a family. But I do have a demanding job, and I do love it. I can't have it all, I guess. But what do I *really* want?" She stopped and began to stretch.

"God can help you figure that out. Look in your heart and find Him."

"Well, I'm sure He knows they offered me a promotion at the office."

"That's great!"

Carter made a face. "More work, is more like it."

It was Gracie's turn to stop. "You've prepared your whole life for this success, Carter. Today's all you can handle, one thing at a time. And the future's always up for revision. Like I said, God is here for you. Your concerns are His own. He knows about your job and your good news, but He cares about you, not the promotion. What's best for you, that is."

She looked fondly at her niece.

"I'd take Don up on his offer."

"He is sweet, isn't he?"

Gracie let her smile be her answer.

It seemed possible that Polly Miller still held answers to some of the questions Gracie had about the key. Her curiosity, in fact, wasn't being encouraged by anyone — well, maybe Marge — but she couldn't manage to stop thinking about it. So she proposed now to Carter that they drive out to Pleasant Haven to visit Polly.

A man was with Polly when Gracie and Carter arrived. As Polly recognized them, he turned around. It was Orville!

Gracie sensed that Hammie's brother felt awkward, as though aware that Gracie knew he was on the outs with Hammie and his wife. Carter introduced herself, trying to put him at ease. Gracie blessed her for her sensitivity.

"Sherry thought you'd gone back to Pennsylvania," Gracie said. "I'm glad to see you haven't."

Orville smiled at his aunt. "I did — or tried to, that is. But then I remembered Aunt Polly, and my promise to spend her birthday with her. I turned around and came back."

"Does Hammie know?" Gracie wanted to know.

He shook his head. "I took a room at Mrs. Fountain's. I'm going to call him later. He's got Sherry's mom there, so it's probably easier this way." Orville frowned. "We didn't part on the best of terms," he admitted.

Gracie noticed her niece studying Orville as he talked.

Upon discovering that she and Carter shared a birthday, Polly was even warmer in her welcome to Gracie's niece. It somehow made meeting someone new an even greater treat. Gracie noticed Orville was watching Carter, too.

"Have you solved your mystery yet?" Polly suddenly thought to ask Gracie.

Gracie stumbled to change the subject, but Polly was too eager to hear what she'd learned since they'd last talked. "I told Orville that you were curious about that key, as well. My hope is that it will clear up a few misunderstandings."

"They're more than misunderstandings, Aunt Polly." Orville looked at her. "I think the key belongs to an unclaimed safe deposit box, the contents of which are being held by the State of Indiana."

Carter looked at Gracie. "In whose name? I checked all the Todd Millers."

"T. S. Miller." Orville corrected her. "My father. But I'm not sure why it's of any interest to you."

Carter glanced at Gracie, who said nothing.

Orville went on, "I think he put the bonds there to keep my mother from inheriting them. I found out he owned some land in Cassidy, too — by the creeks. He may have been planning to use it for a summer place. I know there were serious problems between them. . . ."

"How do you propose to prove this?" Carter asked.

Gracie watched them and was surprised to sense, against all odds, that Carter seemed attracted to the man.

"I thought the key would cinch it, that and some legal papers. But the key is gone."

"You didn't take it?" slipped out of Gracie's mouth before she could stop herself.

Orville stiffened. "Why did you think I did?"

Carter looked worriedly at Polly Miller, willing her to say something to ease the tension.

Gracie suddenly decided to take the bull by the horns. "It's just that it turned up missing right before you left. Did you know anything about the safe deposit box before they found the key in the clock?"

"I saw a database at the Pennsylvania State Fair. The Pennsylvania Attorney General's office had a computer set up, and you could search their files. I figured Indiana must have a similar set-up, and so I began checking. A Mr. T. S. Miller had a safe deposit box containing stock certificates. The problem is, there was no address, and the bank was in a town about an hour from here. Aunt Polly remembers Treasury bonds, but not stocks. And Miller is a common name. So, I wasn't sure if anything I'd found out actually involved my family."

Gracie listened carefully. The confirming connections were still to be made, but what she'd learned on her own seemed to fit in.

"We were discussing all this when you arrived," Aunt Polly told her. "I'm not sure how good our family is at remembering details. But after the key and what you shared with me, Gracie, I began to wonder, could the bonds and the stocks be one and the same?"

"Bonds? Stocks?" Carter glanced first at Polly Miller, then at Orville.

"The unclaimed property is listed as stocks," answered Orville.

Gracie shot Carter a cautioning look. Would her niece tell the man what they knew? She hoped not.

"I don't see that we can file a claim unless we are positive this Miller is our Miller. Without the key, or some other validation, I don't see what we can do."

Orville was glum. "I thought we had something when I saw 'Cassidy' written on the packet. . . ."

"With government agencies," Carter told them, "you have to have all your ducks in a row. They'll just send the paperwork back to you if it isn't complete."

Polly smiled affectionately at her nephew. "Well, if nothing comes of this, so be it. I'm just glad to have Orville back."

"You're wonderful, Aunt Polly." He sounded as if he meant it. "I wish everyone were as accepting as you."

Gracie decided to venture, "Hammie wants to be." If this was out-and-out meddling, so be it. These brothers deserved another chance, and Orville seemed a softer person there in the tender warmth of his aunt's love. Was it only an act?

"Yeah, well, maybe he does, but I don't deserve it."

Now, focusing all his attention on Carter, Orville began to give her what sounded like a carefully edited version of his life. After dropping out of college, he told her he'd ended up roaming Central America, finally finding his place at an experimental farm in Nicaragua.

"It changed my life."

Carter looked at him steadily. "I've always wanted to do something like that, serve in the Peace Corps or volunteer a year in a mission."

"It's impressive that you're a lawyer. Long ago I thought I might be. But I messed up academically," he said, not taking his eyes off her. "Life's full of opportunities, though. I didn't used to think that. Everything seemed so cut and dried, every failure a nail in the coffin. But that's not true. There's always a second chance."

Gracie agreed with what he was saying but felt reluctant to let the man continue flirting with her beloved niece. She took Carter by the arm. "We've got to be going, dear."

"But, Aunt Gracie, you wanted to invite Polly to the fish fry! It will be our birthdays." Carter smiled at Orville. "Of course, you'll come, too?"

"I'd love to."

Gracie swallowed her apprehension. *Lord, I am trusting You on this one!*

14

Gracie worked in the kitchen in silence. Carter would be thirty tomorrow, and Gracie had planned what she'd thought was the perfect early supper. She'd invited Marge, Rocky, Abe and Don Delano. Also, Grover, who was staying with Rocky. But Gracie couldn't put the afternoon behind her. Carter seemed so taken with Orville.

Don joked with Carter while they set the table. But to Gracie's sharp eye, her niece seemed preoccupied. Now she could only hope Carter was once again worried about her workload.

Uncle Miltie and Rocky were wrapping up the checkers game they had started earlier. Marge and Abe were yet to arrive. It had all the makings of a lovely event, one she was going to share with some of the people she loved most in the world. But Orville lingered at the front of her mind. She wondered if Carter was having the same problem.

She wanted to warn her about Hammie's brother, but how could she not see through him? All that blatantly phony talk of service, and putting the needs of others before oneself! Yet how was Carter to know the truth unless Gracie told her? And was Gracie so sure, herself, of what was true?

"Aunt Gracie?" Carter stood in front of her. "Did you hear me? I asked if you wanted me to use paper or cloth napkins."

Gracie pointed to the linens drawer in the dining room sideboard. "I'm glad you chose the good dishes."

"It's a special night." Carter kissed her cheek. "I'm so glad to be here with you this week."

Gracie responded automatically, "What a good idea!"

"Is there something wrong?" Carter asked, almost as if she could read her aunt's mind.

Gracie felt reluctant to explain what she was feeling. How could she tell her niece the problem was she didn't trust Orville? "My mind was on this afternoon. You know me and mysteries."

"I know you," Carter replied. "You give

everyone the benefit of grace. And I love you for it."

Carter hugged her. "I knew you didn't want me to say anything about the patent. I'd trust Orville with the information, but I know it would be harder for you."

Just then Rocky appeared beside them with the crystal water pitcher, to tell her Abe had arrived. Marge opened the back door at the same time. "Hey, everyone!"

"Carter, honey, you look gorgeous!" Marge exclaimed, enveloping her in a hug. Abe appeared behind her, waiting his turn.

Grover pulled out Gracie's chair. "Thanks for including me. As an old bachelor, I don't get much home cooking."

"How was your trip?" He pulled out the chair for Carter. "If I'd known you were coming from Chicago, too, maybe we could have carpooled it."

Uncle Miltie gave a loving grace: "Lord, we thank You for all who have gathered around this table, and for the cook who prepared such a splendid meal. Bless the fellowship of this table, and us to Your service."

Gracie noted that Rocky chorused his "Amen" along with the rest of the company, and she sent up a grateful *Thank You*.

"I want to toast our hostess," Marge said,

holding up her glass of water. "She's the best."

Gracie knew how both to accept a compliment and how to turn it into praise for others. "I love my friends and they inspire me. If I have any claim on being 'best,' it's only because they make me that way. Praise the Lord."

Quickly, conversation slipped into comfortable small talk, until Grover asked about the key. Gracie filled him in on the latest developments.

"It seems that either Todd or Samuel registered a patent," Carter summarized. "And that patent looks to have generated a huge amount of money, more than the inventors could have imagined."

Grover offered, "You know, Franklin always said Todd had a real intuitive mechanical mind."

Carter put her fork down. "Regarding Todd, we don't know anything for sure. A T. S. Miller filed the patent with a company called Willspring, we *do* know that."

"Wills — for Franklin Wills." Grover was excited. "It's got to be!"

"What it looks like is that they got investors to back it. Then there was an initial stock purchase, and those stocks sat in that safe deposit box. Eventually, the company was swallowed by a bigger one, making the stocks valuable."

Rocky looked at Carter. "And how does Orville fit into all this?"

"I don't know, but I hope to find out." Carter smiled. "He's taking me out for ice cream, after the Sweet Adelines' practice."

Uncle Miltie whistled. "Pretty quick work."

"It's not a date!" Carter declared. "He called her earlier, and I just happened to pick up the phone. He said he'd been thinking about our conversation at Pleasant Haven. Maybe I can be of some real help. Like Aunt Gracie, I'm intrigued by mysteries."

Gracie took a deep breath. "Just remember, dear. People aren't always as they seem."

"No, they're not," Carter agreed.

Estelle had chosen a medley of hauntingly beautiful folk music, including some old Scottish hymns, for the Sweet Adelines. And, as could be expected, she'd selected each piece to best showcase their range of voices. Barb was more than willing to heap praise on her.

As a result, Estelle was in her glory. "Mother was always so disappointed that she couldn't provide more financing for my music education. But she was convinced, as she liked to say, that my day would come. Well, Gracie, it's here! I love doing this!"

"And, when it comes to the choir, it takes a burden off Barb's shoulders," Gracie declared. "You are both blessed."

Barb, hearing this, added, "And isn't that just the way with God, blessing us when we help others?"

"Indeed." Gracie glanced to the back of the church, where Orville stood waiting for Carter.

Marge came over to her side. "Don's still my first choice."

"Mine, too," Gracie admitted. "But Orville and she are just going for ice cream."

"We could go for ice cream, too," Marge suggested. "Incognito. We could slip in that back booth and spy on them."

Gracie reminded her friend. "Carter can take care of herself. Besides, we'd look pretty funny in wigs and big sunglasses and people going, 'Yoo-hoo, Gracie! Marge!' "

"We'd just claim we forgot what month Halloween was in!"

Gracie laughed. But her heart was heavier than it should have been after making such beautiful music with friends.

Hammie was just locking up the feed store when Gracie and Marge pulled up. "What brings you ladies to these premises? It's late."

"We called your house on my cell phone, and Sherry said you were still here checking inventory."

"There's always more to do than I can get done. Plus, sometimes I just need time to think. And Sherry and her mother can have even more time together this way."

"It is certainly exciting and a big, big life change," Gracie told him.

"Well, I know, but I'm going be the best dad I can be." Hammie gave them a proud smile. "But what can I do for you?"

Marge looked at Gracie, who wasn't sure where to begin.

"You probably already know that Orville is staying at Cordelia's," Hammie said, taking the lead. "He called me at the store to apologize, and we agreed this was probably the better arrangement, what with Sherry's mother here and all."

He paused. "I guess we can't expect things to change overnight. Orville's always gone his own way. I expect I'll find out what's on his mind soon enough."

Gracie told them about their visit to his Aunt Polly. "I understand it's really not my concern. But I thought you should know. Please don't think me a busybody."

"Gracie, I'd never think that. It's just that I'm always hoping Orville will be different. I hadn't seen him in almost ten years, since before Grandpa died. When he called, I was pleased. He's my brother and I missed him. One forgets the bad parts after time. I haven't wanted to think he just came back for more money — not again."

Gracie was afraid that that was exactly why Orville had returned. But she decided to put her optimism ahead of her worry. "Your Aunt Polly believes he wants to share the inheritance with you, once it's proved the rightful claimant is your family."

"The thing I don't understand is, if my father and Franklin owned the company, how did my grandfather get involved? And why Cassidy?"

Marge told him, "We hoped maybe you could answer that."

"It looks like your father and Franklin Wills had a connection to a fish hatchery in Cassidy," Gracie explained. "It seems to be where they tested a prototype of the pump they were working on."

"Grover is going to check," Marge added.

"After all, he has an interest in getting to the bottom of this, as well."

"The odd thing is that Willspring was absorbed by a larger company in 1986."

"It doesn't make sense. I was at college then. And Orville was still in high school — no, he would have graduated by then."

"Did he go to college?"

Hammie nodded. "He thought he'd study law eventually, but then he switched to science. We weren't close. He ended up dropping out. He never gave a reason, just came home disillusioned and bent on going off to find himself. He wanted his share of our inheritance. He and Grandpa had a big fight over it, but he finally gave Orville the money. Then he took off."

Gracie tried to sort it out in her mind. "So your grandfather had those Treasury bonds? That would have been the inheritance, right?"

"I don't know where the money came from, except I know that Grandpa put it in a trust for us." Hammie scratched his head. "Of course, I tried not to pay much attention. I just didn't want to get in the middle of their battle."

"Money seems to bring out the worst in people," Marge said. "It's an old idea that's always new. Unfortunately."

"It wasn't easy that Grandpa was pitting me against my brother. Orville hated me at that time: I was the 'good son.' " Hammie looked at Gracie. "I just love this place. And I never wanted anything but to live here and work in the store.

"Orville accused me of pandering to Grandpa. Grandpa knew I would never leave Willow Bend, but he pushed and pushed for a promise right in front of Orville. He made me sign documents swearing that I wouldn't sell after he died. I tried to reason with him all the rest of his life, figuring the will could set things right. Otherwise, Orville would never forgive me, even if he'd already gotten that lump sum."

"So Orville didn't receive anything from your grandfather's estate?"

Hammie shook his head. "I think Grandpa thought I was weak, that I'd give in to Orville and sell the store. There was a clause in that paper I signed that stated I could make the decision to share his inheritance, so long as I didn't sell the property."

Hammie shook his head. "Orville had been gone for years when Grandpa died, and I didn't have an address to contact him. He called one night, and we got into a terrible fight. I said some pretty hard things, and he accused me of cheating him out of his inheritance. I couldn't tell him what Grandpa had done, so I promised to make it right. I had the estate appraised, and gave him half. I never showed him Grandpa's will. And I'd appreciate if that stays between us."

Marge spoke up. "You're an amazing man, Hammie Miller. I know your mother would have thought so, too. You're a lot like her."

Gracie now suspected that Orville might have learned the true nature of the inheritance after he showed up in Willow Bend. Hammie confirmed that Orville had been to the courthouse, and to see his grandfather's lawyer.

"But he never said anything to you about what he'd learned? Never acknowledged your extraordinary generosity and love?"

"No. We didn't really talk about it. I guess I was afraid to bring it up. I just wanted everything to be all right. Maybe it's a guy thing. He told us about working in Central America. He told us he'd spent some time in Africa, too. I didn't want to pry, and he didn't offer a lot.

"Sherry suspected he was ashamed. She suspected he might even have been making things up, just to explain all those missing

195

years. But, Gracie, I didn't want to embarrass him."

Hammie thought a moment, then sighed. "I guess it's about time we really sat down and talked. Maybe it will be easier, now that he's staying at Cordelia's."

Gracie prayed it could happen. Rehashing past grievances would never get them anywhere. Now, if they could just be honest with one another and move forward.

"I think that's why I suggested the fishing weekend," Hammie told them. "I figured there was safety in numbers and that we could avoid the inevitable. I never wanted to cheat my brother out of anything, Gracie. But I'm not sure what's happening now."

"Hammie," Gracie said softly, "I'm going to be praying for you both."

Uncle Miltie had apparently turned in early. A steady snore and whistle attested to it. Carter was still out. Gracie washed the few dishes in the sink, fixed herself a cup of hot cocoa and glanced at the clock. Almost eleven.

The day had been disconcerting, but all still was not right with her world.

Gracie tried to forget her sense of foreboding. She thumbed through the new issue of *Guideposts*, hoping for something to take her mind off Carter and Orville. Two issues and a second cup of cocoa later, she heard the front door open. It was now midnight.

"Aunt Gracie!" Carter started as she entered the kitchen. "I thought somebody'd left the lights on. Why aren't you in bed?"

Gracie managed a smile. "I guess you never stop being the parent. I always waited up for Arlen."

"Thank you." She kissed her aunt on the forehead.

"I really don't want to pry but, Carter, are you convinced Orville Miller is someone you wish to spend time with?"

"We were just walking." Carter got the milk from the refrigerator and warmed a cupful in the microwave. "We got an ice cream cone, and it was a nice starlit night, so we walked to the park and sat and talked." She took the seat across from Gracie.

"Orville's really nice, Aunt Gracie. And interesting, too. He's really been out in the world doing things, not just sitting behind a desk."

She went on to explain how he'd been working with experimental farm projects around the world. "Honest, Aunt Gracie, can't you just see how it's a case of the apple not falling far from the tree? He's more like his grandfather than he'd ever admit. And a lot like his father and brother, too — but, at the same time, he's *himself*."

Carter teased her aunt now. "And those gray eyes — kind of stormy, a little moody, but imploring. Remember I said I seemed to prefer men who presented more of a challenge?"

Gracie remembered all too well. "Well, let's challenge him about what he intends to do with any funds he recovers, if they exist."

Carter had an answer for this. "He says he wants to give most of it to Hammie, to pay him back. The rest he'd use to pay off loans and then he has this farm in Nicaragua he wants to back."

"But why wasn't he honest with Hammie?" Gracie still was uneasy about Orville's motivations. Had she been wrong all along? Was he simply a prickly fellow but one who intended to do the right thing all along?

"I didn't tell him what I know, so maybe I, too, am a little hesitant to trust him completely," said Carter. "I really like him, though. I think he's telling me the truth — even if it's edited a little. And he did admit that he went through a rebellious period, and did a lot of things that he's ashamed of."

Gracie reached for her niece's hand. "I just don't want you to get hurt."

"I know. But don't worry. Orville and I are only new friends. I'm going back to Chicago, and he's going back to Pennsylvania."

Carter looked at Gracie with a level gaze. "I sense he needs an advocate right now. He's sure everyone's against him. His Aunt Polly is the only real reason he's staying. And even her love for him came as a surprise. He didn't expect anyone to care. He knows they have good reason to dislike him. And to distrust him."

Gracie conceded, "Orville's been hurt, that's apparent."

"Well, he lost both parents. He recognizes his behavior has been self-destructive, but he's trying to turn his life around."

Gracie hoped Carter was right. She wanted to believe her.

But only time would tell.

15

Her gang of male friends had the preparations for the evening's fish fry well under way when Gracie arrived in the church kitchen the next afternoon. Smells of creamy potatoes and cheese, spicy batter dip and fresh cole slaw filled the kitchen. She kissed her aproned uncle on the cheek, praised everything she could think of, and put the coconut sheet cake that she'd baked early that morning before church on the counter.

"Thank you, my dear. You're my inspiration, of course."

The kitchen crew drew around to admire the cake Gracie had baked and Marge had decorated. "That may not look like a row of fish lined up along a lakeside, but she decided not to try to depict the less dramatic wholesale fish delivery!" Gracie told them.

"Oh, look!" said Les. "Each fish has a little bell! Kind of hard to ring them with fins!"

As Gracie now helped Grover with the set-ups, he filled her in on some new pieces of the puzzle. "Todd and Franklin did, in fact, together own Willspring Equipment. My brother's signature is on the buyout documents, but Franklin and Sam signed all the other paperwork. Sam apparently inherited that part of Todd's estate. Why, is a mystery. I did find out that the stocks are actually in Orville's and Hammie's names. Sam set it up that way."

Gracie looked at him in surprise. "Okay, but why in a safe deposit box in Cassidy?"

"That I don't know. But I've got a theory. Sam obviously knew about the pump in Cassidy — he and Franklin set up the endowment. Maybe he went there to check it out. Maybe he put the papers in the box. I did learn that Todd in fact rented a box. Sam inherited the contents.

"I'm going to stop in Cassidy on the way back to Chicago. I'll call Rocky when I know more." Grover looked thoughtful. "We'll get to the bottom of this yet."

Rocky had overheard. "I told Grover what the old timer in Cassidy said about the fish farm. It was easy enough to check up on, and they did use the pump designed by Willspring."

"I'm starting to realize how important it is to have your estate in order," Gracie now said. "None of this might have seemed so mysterious if Todd Miller had had a will."

Grover nodded. "Nobody likes drafting a will. For the obvious reasons. I had Franklin's Power of Attorney. Not something you want to find yourself executing for a sibling."

"Or a spouse." Gracie and Rocky both could empathize.

Rocky changed the subject. "Would you say there's a budding romance between Carter and Orville?"

"I hope not!" Gracie couldn't hide her concern. "But something about him appeals to her, and it doesn't have to make any sense."

"She has a good head on her shoulders, you know that," Rocky reminded her. "Orville's a loner, that's for sure. If he's opened up to Carter, then that says something for his good sense, despite everything we've seen."

Grover remembered how Orville had kept to himself at the cabin, preferring to spend the time sorting through his grandfather's belongings. "I don't think he fished at all up at the cabin that weekend, did he? Or hung out with any of you?"

"That's what I mean — the guy's a loner. I felt a little sorry for him."

"He got excited once," Grover recalled. "Uncle Miltie saw a hummingbird, and Orville told us that they were unique to the New World. He's been pretty much a vagabond, moving around from one country to the next."

Rocky agreed. "I told him that I'd lived in Colombia, and he told me a little about his Nicaraguan experiences. He's hard to read, I admit, and has a lot of resentments. But maybe he's just one of those personalities that rub people the wrong way."

"I had a boss like that. Abrasive as sandpaper, but a straight shooter. He'd stand by his men when the chips were down." Grover chuckled. "I guess it only goes to prove you can't judge the man by the scowl he wears."

Carter's observations weren't so different. Gracie shared with them what her niece had told her.

"Most of the time, though, Orville was pretty tight-lipped out at the cabin," Rocky said. "I guess he opens up only when you hit a subject that interests him. Otherwise, it's pretty much monosyllables all the way."

Grover agreed. "Made me more than a

little suspicious about his motives. You could call it an occupational hazard."

"That's why I insisted that Hammie hold on to the key," Rocky said. "The fact that I couldn't get a clear reading on him meant I wanted to wait and let Orville *prove* I could trust him."

She glanced over to where her niece was talking to Orville, who'd just arrived, pushing his aunt in her wheelchair. *Lord, look out for her heart, for me, please. And help me see this young man with Your eyes.*

"You all ready for your big debut later on?" Pastor Paul asked, joining them by the tables.

Gracie introduced Grover.

Pastor Paul gave him a warm handshake. "It's really wonderful what you've accomplished in a little over a week. And Lester tells me that this event may just bring in more than half of the needed funds!"

He turned to Rocky. "I'm so glad to have our illustrious editor here, too! Maybe we'll see you around here more often? Like on Sunday mornings?"

Rocky, as was rarely the case, seemed suddenly at a loss for words.

Gracie couldn't help remembering Rocky comparing going to church with wearing a necktie: You had to button up the neck to look presentable, but you looked forward to popping it open at the first opportunity.

"Think about joining us," Pastor Paul told him. "You know we'd love to have you. And so would the Lord. But, of course, He even loves errant newspapermen when they go fishing on Sundays. That's just the way He is."

Gracie knew when she wasn't needed, and sat down to enjoy the delicious meal with Carter, Marge, Polly and Orville. She took second helpings of the crispy fried fish and the creamy cole slaw.

"I thought maybe you'd be helping in the kitchen," Gracie told Orville, who also seemed to be eating heartily.

He shrugged. "Not sure anyone wanted me there."

"Nonsense!" Polly declared. "Orville, it's time to get that chip off your shoulder! Today's a new day, and folks here are more than willing to give you a second chance."

Carter laughed. "You tell him, Miss Miller!" She focused on Orville. "She's right, you know, about its being a new beginning. You've turned your life around. Let people meet the Orville I've already gotten to know."

"You and Hammie are going to make up,

205

if I have anything to say about it." Polly shook her finger. "If you won't talk to him, I will."

Polly turned to Gracie. "Sherry was feeling a little tired and not exactly up to fried food, so they didn't come. I know they're planning to be here in time for the program, though. And Orville is going to apologize — no ifs, ands or buts about it. There's not a better thing they can give me for my birthday."

The old woman smiled. "That's one of the best benefits of being old — everyone has to humor you."

Even Orville had to smile at this.

Backstage, excitement practically bubbled over as the singers assembled.

"Well, here we are!" Rocky said jauntily, as he came up beside her.

She took him in, from straw hat to pinstriped vest and saddle shoes. "Don't you look dapper!"

Rocky tipped his hat with his walking stick. "Why, thank you, ma'am."

Barb tapped her baton, and the audience held its breath in happy anticipation.

"I'm a little nervous," Marybeth said. "Usually we have a lot more time to rehearse. And a choir's more safely anonymous, somehow."

"But they're all our friends out there," Gracie reminded her.

Marybeth laughed. "And my children! They warned me about getting too close to the microphone. They're so afraid I'm going to embarrass them during my solo part."

"Kids are embarrassed by just about anything when it comes to their parents," Gracie said. "It goes with the territory."

"Positions, positions!" This was for the Adelines. The men stood in the wings. Gracie sensed the sigh of relief that they hadn't drawn the first spotlight. The bell choir would end the evening, as the pièce de résistance.

"You ready?" Carter slipped her arm through Gracie's.

"Happy birthday, darling," Gracie whispered. "I'll bet you've never had one like this before!"

"Nor soon will I again!" Carter winked.

"Did you see where Orville went?" her niece asked Gracie after the performance. All three segments had been carried off with gusto, and Gracie would never forget the sight of Rocky crooning away lustily, waggling his cane. The bells had sent both ringers and spectators into an ecstasy of pleasure. The sounds would echo in her ears for a long time to come, Gracie knew.

Gracie turned to Carter. She hadn't seen Orville leave, but she noticed his aunt nearby. "Why don't you ask Polly?"

Gracie now scanned the church hall, spotting Sherry and her mother, but no Hammie. Perhaps the brothers had decided to go off and talk, finally.

Pastor Paul suddenly stood up and clapped his hands. "I've just heard from Orville Miller that today is an important day. Let's sing 'Happy Birthday' to Polly Miller, ninety years young, and Carter Stephens, whose age . . . ?" he grinned sheepishly. "I know better than to ask."

"Thanks!" Carter called.

"That's my girl," Gracie said. "You look pleased all of a sudden to be hitting this milestone!"

Carter grinned. "With such fabulous role models, how can I be any other way?" She reached to squeeze Polly's hand. "Happy birthday!"

As they sang "Happy Birthday," Rocky and Abe wheeled a cart carrying Gracie's cake, blazing with candles, out of the kitchen. Orville appeared beside them with two packages.

Gracie glanced around the room and now

saw Hammie sitting with Sherry and his mother-in-law.

Orville spoke. "Most of you know me, and those who don't — well, maybe I'm thankful."

He paused a moment. "I've done a lot of stupid things in my life. But returning to Willow Bend isn't one of them. I am very glad to be home.

"I thought it was going to be the hardest thing I ever did, last week, when I arrived in town. I'd taken it for granted that things were going to go badly. I had a lot for which to be sorry. And I owed more than money could compensate to my brother and aunt.

"Of course, at that time I didn't know it. Like my aunt says, I've got a chip on my shoulder the size of Mason County." He smiled fondly at her. "Actually, she said I hadn't changed a bit. So, another thing about turning ninety, Aunt Polly, your eyesight isn't what it used to be!"

Gracie couldn't believe her ears. Around her everyone else was listening intently, as well.

Orville looked past his aunt to his brother. "There's really nothing I can offer Aunt Polly for her birthday but an apology . . . to my brother. That's what she wants and what I want to give her. And him.

"Hammie is one of the best human beings I know. He's afforded me more grace than I deserve. It's hard to come home with your tail between your legs, but Hammie didn't just meet me at the door, he ran to my car. He threw his arms around me before I even had a chance to say I was sorry. And I just want to say . . . I'm sorry."

Hammie pushed his chair back, and ran to embrace his brother to the sound of thunderous applause.

Gracie noticed she wasn't the only one wiping away a tear.

16

Blair Mills Preserve was postcard pretty, with waves of marsh grass and clusters of vivid wildflowers stretching for acres. Gracie savored the sweet, mild breeze as she strolled with Carter and Rocky along the brick walkway lined with brightly colored perennials. These represented the region's common, and also its endangered, flora. Above them they heard the high-pitched chatter of birds, warning of the approach of interlopers. Gracie felt almost apologetic for disturbing the serenity there.

Carter slipped her arm around Gracie's waist. "Thank you, Aunt Gracie," she whispered.

"My dear," Gracie said. "I so enjoy your company. You are the daughter I never had. I'm going to thank your mother for sharing you with me."

Carter hugged her. "I love you, Aunt Gracie. I'm so glad I took an extra couple of days to stay longer with you. I needed this time, I really did. And you knew I did."

They walked in companionable silence, each lost in pleasant recollection. Gracie recalled the celebration at the church. Orville had handed his aunt a gift-wrapped journal of what he called his "prodigal year," explaining his long journey back home.

"Orville has turned out to be an exceptional man," she said aloud.

"You must have read my mind. I was just thinking about him. You know, you were right. He confessed to me that he had first come back to Willow Bend to find proof that those stocks or bonds belonged to him. He felt cheated by Hammie. And then he learned the truth."

Gracie paused by the flower beds to listen to Carter. Rocky walked on ahead. "But what of his apology?"

"Oh, he meant it. That's the point. Coming here changed his mind. His Aunt Polly embraced him like a long-lost son. He was so ashamed, but she wouldn't hear of it, saying that she was just happy to have him home. He had brought that journal with him for moral support.

"It was about his time abroad and the year

he spent in Nicaragua. He realized as he re-read it that envy and bitterness had short-circuited his ambitions. In seeking revenge against his grandfather, he had sabotaged his own best interests. I mean, he flunked out of college just to spite him!"

Carter went on to tell Gracie that she had encouraged him to give the journal to both Polly and Hammie to read. But sharing it with his brother was still too intimidating, so he wrote his brother a letter instead.

"More of an apology than an explanation. Orville said writing it down helped him. He hadn't realized how much of a role jealousy had played in his self-destructive behavior. I know he still struggles with it, but this is surely a beginning."

Carter smiled. "You know, really, Aunt Gracie, Orville is one of those cream fillings you always have told me about. His crustiness was just a cover-up for hurt."

"And he did a brave thing," Gracie acknowledged. "He faced his past and 'fessed up to some embarrassing things. The birthday you and Polly shared turned out to be very special for her, too."

"It was a conspiracy." Carter laughed. "She phoned me and thanked me for inviting Orville. It was her call that prompted me to encourage Orville. She believed in him, Gracie. And she wanted those brothers to come together, more than anything else."

Gracie said softly, "God does work all things for good, for those who love Him."

They walked arm in arm past an aquarium housing native fish to the hatch house and rearing ponds. They headed across a wooden boardwalk to the observation platform, where Grover and their host waited for them at the spillway to the creek and small lake beyond.

John Higgins extended his hand first to Gracie, then Rocky. He addressed the editor. "Mr. Wills has told me a lot about you. So, you're going to do a story on our experimental farm?"

Rocky shot his friend a quizzical look.

"I knew you would want to do a story as soon as you saw this place. It's a fishery trust, part of a global effort to ensure sustainable fishing in the future. Is that a great story, or what?"

Grover flashed Rocky a sheepish grin. "Besides, it makes your drive worthwhile."

Rocky groused a moment, but decided it did seem a good story, considering the local angle and the recent discovery that Sam Miller had endowed the project.

John asked about the drive, and Grover updated them on what he'd learned since arriving at the preserve a day earlier. "I had only intended to make a short stop before heading back home, but I got here and was fascinated. I'm amazed my brother never told me about it! I knew you had to see it for yourselves."

"Your brother and Mr. Miller made this possible. Without their investment, Blair Mills Preserve would have been a pipe dream. Their electric aerator provided not only an efficient system for getting oxygen to the bottom of these ponds, but the capital to keep the research going. We're indebted to those men."

The environmentalist pointed to two small windmills connected to a crankshaft, and connecting rods and hoses leading into the ponds. "We use those to get oxygen to the bottom of the tanks and pools. It's very important not only to get the oxygen to the surface, but also to the bottom as well, so that new larvae, snails and other fish food can thrive. Todd Miller's ingenuity made that possible."

"It turns out," Grover went on, "those Treasury bonds in the Cassidy bank were collateral on the loan to finish the venture. A local friend had the dream, and all three men shared a passion for fishing and the environment."

Grover filled them in on the particulars. Fred Spring, the owner of the land, was also the proprietor of a lawn-equipment franchise. He and Todd got to know each other at the county fair, where their booths were side by side. It was Fred's idea to restock the streams.

It seemed chemicals had leached from a large mill and had caused environmental damage to the streams running through the large tract. Fred purchased the land with the intent to restore and preserve it for community enjoyment.

"These were some of the state's most pristine trout streams," John told them. "But a century of industrialization has taken its toll. We are working to clean it up, but the fish stock was so depleted, some varieties were almost extinct."

Grover moved closer to the older cement tanks. "Fred built these himself. They were his first project. He didn't know much about engines or pumps, but he knew he had to have an aerator. It's almost the same system that's used in aquariums. Just makes for a healthier environment."

John pointed to the hose leading from the windmill. "Pumping compressed air into the deep water creates bubbles, and pushes bad gases to the surface. Aeration speeds up the oxidizing — or burning up — of pollutants, creating the nutrient-rich, clear, sweet-smelling water we have here. And it ensures future crops of healthy fish, plankton and other food organisms. It's a complete system."

"Todd had a knack for mechanics. He'd spent his youth working on lawnmowers and small gas engines. And Franklin was a design person. He used both his architectural skills and his conservation savvy to plan the whole system," Grover said.

Gracie looked at Grover. "And you didn't know anything about this project?"

"I knew he came fishing here. I remembered that it was the place where he often met Todd. But, no, I was busy establishing my career with the government. If he told me anything, I glossed over it, like I did most of his fish talk. The guy was a true fanatic."

Gracie watched the small fish in the tank in front of her.

"Chinook," John told her. "This is a rearing pond. We are quite proud to be part of the Great Lakes program for restocking native salmon."

Grover tucked his hands under his arms and grinned. "I just wanted you guys to see this place. I feel it's almost like having

Franklin back again. I hate to sound goofy, but I really can feel his spirit here!"

"Grover, believe me," Gracie assured him, "you loved your brother, that's not goofy at all!"

"And see how Orville took his love of the land and nature that he inherited, and put it into farming techniques," Carter reminded them. "That's Todd's spirit manifesting itself, too."

"I really want the brothers to see this," Grover agreed. He turned to Rocky. "You said they would be right behind you?"

"I called Orville on his cell phone," Carter offered. "He and Hammie wanted to walk around the old farm outside of town. They had a lot of talking to do, and so they'll come over here later. I think they want to be alone."

John excused himself, telling Grover he'd be in his office if they needed him.

"I see you're not only a prosecutor, but also a first-class mediator, as well." Grover touched Carter's arm. "You didn't let Orville's reputation get in the way of friendship. You gave him the benefit of the doubt. And you listened to him."

Gracie sighed silently, remembering how Patty and Franklin had suffered because folks were not willing to give them the benefit of the doubt. She swallowed her own guilt at not being as generous about Orville as her niece had been.

She hugged her niece. "I'm proud of you."

Rocky smiled. "I hope you'll forgive me, Carter, if I said I'm still not entirely sure about how much he can be trusted."

"I understand your apprehension. Orville admitted to me that at first, he'd wanted only restitution for what he thought he'd been cheated out of. He was going to claim all that money and say nothing. But, then, he read a copy of his grandfather's will."

Gracie understood how traumatic that would have been. Hammie had inherited everything. Contrary to what Hammie had told his brother, there had been no codicil about holding on to the assets until Orville had matured. Hammie could have told him to take a hike when he demanded his share. So, he had discovered the truth — Hammie was really his benefactor.

"Orville's ashamed and angry. Gosh, parents can do so much damage, even from the grave. He only wanted his grandfather's love, really. He still envies Hammie that."

Grover turned to face them. "But he had his grandfather's love! The stocks are in Orville's name. I understand there are some legal documents and a letter. But he's going to have to claim them. Has someone explained all this to him?"

"I asked a lawyer friend to help," Carter said. "But how do you know all this?"

Grover grinned. "Working for the government has its privileges. Let's just say I have an inside source."

"So, you're saying Sam left some of the stocks to Orville?" Gracie remembered how Polly had known the truth — his grandfather had loved him too much. "He put them in a safe deposit box in Cassidy?"

"And the key?" Rocky wanted to know.

Carter shook her head. "Orville didn't take it."

Grover finished his story. It seemed Franklin had contacted Sam when North American Equipment approached him about buying the patent. Sam came to Cassidy to see the project, and learned what happened to the Treasury bonds. He claimed what was left of the collateral, and he and Franklin agreed to establish a trust to preserve the project with the sales from the buyout of Todd's and Franklin's patent. However, they were also given stock options.

"And I assume that those stock options were in the safe deposit box. Why here in

Cassidy, only Sam could tell us."

Gracie couldn't help thinking, "Sam was sentimental. He wouldn't wind that clock, so it would be just like him to put the key there, too."

Rocky was quick to suggest lunch at Lou's Diner, and Grover seconded the motion. The pair seemed have the same taste in cuisine, heavy on the greasy stuff and light on the green vegetables. Gracie knew El would have liked Grover, as well. He had an easygoing nature and a quick intelligence that informed his sturdy character.

"Hey, it's the fighting fisherman!" Shirley called to Rocky, as he walked into the diner with his three friends.

Grover laughed. "What have you been telling this woman? If I know you, Old Hammerhead grew three sizes between the boat and this bar."

"Nah, he's too modest to brag." Shirley winked. "And cute to boot. So, what'll you have, good looking?" She said to Grover, who blushed and ducked behind his menu.

Gracie detected a hint of sage in the wafting aroma of sausage and milk gravy. "The special smells good."

"Just a couple of servings left." Shirley glanced toward the kitchen. "The sausage gravy's good — best in the state, they tell me." She turned back to them, and grinned. "And the biscuits? Why, today they're almost edible."

They listened to Shirley's cheery whistling as she fixed the sausage and gravy for Grover and Rocky, and bacon, lettuce and tomato club sandwiches for Carter and Gracie.

Gracie, after she'd finished her lunch, decided to ask Shirley something. "That's quite a project out at Blair Mills, and beautiful recreation spot. You all must be proud of it."

"Can't say as I've been out there." Shirley poured refills of coffee. "I guess that's how it is. Folks take for granted what's in the backyard. It's a popular fishing area, though."

She grinned at the guys. "Judging by the tales I hear, more fish are taken out of those streams than were ever put in."

"I can believe that!" Grover chuckled. "Swapping stories is half the fun of it. Spinning fish yarns was second nature to my brother."

"It puts to practical use all those long mornings waiting for something to bite," Rocky theorized. "You have to have something to show for all that time sitting still."

Shirley's expression turned serious. "You know, I wanted to tell you about Todd

Miller when you here the last time, but some things are best left unsaid — especially in front of local ears. If we'd have been alone in the diner the day you two dropped in, I would have shared the rest of the story.

"Todd and I went through too many pots of coffee here, him telling me about his un-happiness," Shirley said. "It wasn't easy. He was a good-looking guy, and he chose me to confide in."

Gracie held her breath.

"It was me who urged him to go back to his wife — to make a fresh start. He's had a falling-out with her. That's why he took out the safety deposit box. He was in the middle of some big deal and was going to keep everything secret. His friend tried to talk him out of it — and so did I. But he was mad at his wife. I don't know why."

She looked at Gracie. "That's why I told you about that newspaper ad. I was tempted to claim it. Todd was dead. I knew he took out that box to protect some of his assets. I wrestled with it, believe me, I did. But I couldn't have shown my face in church if I would have done what I was conniving. God spared me that humiliation. I called Todd's father. I told him about the box."

Gracie touched Shirley's arm. "You did the right thing."

"I know. I cried when I heard he'd died. Todd loved his wife. I told him to call her and apologize. I just hope he finally did. Todd resisted feeling like he was tied down — but I can tell you, he did love his family."

Shirley cleared her throat, clearly struggling with emotion. "I just thought you ought to know all that. Funny, how the past comes back to haunt a person."

"Maybe not so much to haunt but to encourage — to heal." Gracie blinked back tears. She looked around at her companions.

Grover was apparently lost in recollections of his own. Rocky, too, seemed far away. Gracie glanced at Carter, who had remained quiet.

"I guess that's what they mean when they talk about the wisdom of experience," Carter said softly. "Everybody makes mistakes. We ought to be thankful for the opportunities to correct them. God is good that way, isn't He, Aunt Gracie?"

Gracie nodded. "He surely is."

Marge was right — the past did have a way of ambushing a person. But grace triumphed in the long run, and the future looked brighter because of it. Shirley understood that. And Gracie was confident

Hammie and Orville would soon have time on their side too.

Gracie returned to ladling soup for the trio at her kitchen table.

Carter nodded. "People talk about fresh starts, and moving on — but that really can't happen until we face our mistakes. Wisdom comes in understanding that."

Marge smiled. "It's all a matter of attitude. When I look in the mirror of my mind, well, let's say I still see the schoolgirl."

"Some of us have been pressing an age so long it's been pleated," Uncle Miltie teased. "Forget the exercise and diet, I'm just going to borrow that mirror, Marge."

Marge's eyes twinkled. "Close your eyes, my friend, and I know you'll see the George Morgan who could leap tall buildings at a single bound!"

Carter laughed. "This has been the best birthday!"

Uncle Miltie banged his spoon on his bowl. "Hear! Hear!"

Finished ladling the soup, Gracie sat down.

Uncle Miltie reached for Gracie's and Carter's hands on either side of him. "Let's return thanks." Marge bowed her head.

Gracie breathed deeply as her uncle

thanked God for the blessings of friends and family, and asked traveling mercy for Carter. He ended by reminding them all that God was in their midst.

"... Let all we say be honoring to You."

"Amen," they all repeated.

When they walked Carter to her car to say goodbye, Orville was there, waiting in his own vehicle. Carter waved him into the group, but Gracie sensed his hesitation. She smiled, beckoning him to the driveway.

Carter promised a return visit soon, causing Uncle Miltie to start fussing over her again. Marge, her earrings jangling, ran home to get Charlotte, then made them all pose for a group picture, Gooseberry included.

Orville seemed content to stay at the edge of the circle. But he watched with a pleasant, relaxed expression on his face.

Gracie kissed her niece again, and Carter called to Orville that she would phone him from Chicago. They waved goodbye, and Gracie swallowed her sadness.

"How about dessert?" she asked, as Carter drove off.

Marge hugged Gracie tightly. "Chicago is not the end of the earth. You and I are going to take that trip — soon!"

"I know, but I miss her already."

"That'll make our next reunion all the fonder."

Uncle Miltie rubbed his hands together. "So, did someone say dessert?"

Orville turned to leave.

"We'd love to have you stay," Gracie told him.

His smile showed that he understood she meant it.

Marge, slipping her arm in his, promised to share her memories of his mother with him. At that moment, Rocky pulled up — always in time for dessert, Gracie noted.

Gracie waited for Rocky. "We've been having quite an adventure, haven't we?" she said to him, with a welcoming smile.

It was Uncle Miltie who, at the kitchen table, braved the subject of the missing key.

"Hammie was sure he put it in the tray, and I want to believe him," Orville said. "But it's gone. Somebody had to have taken it, but it wasn't me."

Rocky cut himself a second piece of gingerbread. Gracie handed him the dish of whipped cream. "You only live once," he reminded her before turning his attention to Orville. "So, the key's still missing?"

"I really thought Hammie had it, and was avoiding confrontation by saying that it was lost. That would be like him, avoiding the problem, hoping maybe it will disappear."

Orville paused. "But I don't think that any more. I believe him when he says that he's searched and searched for it. He seems as mystified as the rest of us."

"The Bermuda Triangle," Uncle Miltie said. "That's where it is."

Gracie took the seat beside Orville. "How long are you going stay in town?"

"Long enough to settle things with the stocks. I'm glad things are out in the open now. I'm pretty broke. But I've got a home in Central America, and I want to go back. I want Hammie to have his due, and then, if there's anything left . . . well, there's a farm in Nicaragua that could use that money."

He looked at Gracie. "I was telling the truth about my experience there. Carter is considering giving it a summer of her time. But whatever she decides doesn't change my commitment. And I know I always have a place here in Willow Bend to return to."

Gracie knew when she'd been praying in the right direction. God's love was in Orville — but, then again, it always had been. Her heart leapt. *Thank You.*

Gracie was putting her groceries in her car just as Ellen and Sherry pulled into the parking space next to hers at the Willow

Mart. Sherry greeted her, bubbling with enthusiasm for everything Hammie had told her about the preserve and his father's legacy.

"We're going to plan a picnic there one Sunday before the baby comes," Sherry told her. "John Higgins says they would like to have a rededication ceremony. And Mr. Gravino says he's doing a story on it. It's all so wonderful! I can put the clippings in our baby book."

Gracie was warmed by the glow of her enthusiasm. It had been a short journey for her and Hammie out to Cassidy, but a long journey lay ahead to their future. They were embarked on a trip that Gracie knew only too well, one whose every precious minute she cherished.

Sherry looked at Gracie. "Dr. Wright has given us a clean bill of health. Everything looks fine, God willing. Hammie and I are excited. And Orville, you know, he seems excited, too. He's been a lot different lately. Aunt Polly's so proud of him, ever since that night at church." Sherry glanced at her mom.

Ellen looked less convinced.

"Well, I, for one, have grown to have a much higher opinion of your brother-in-law," Gracie declared. "How's it going between them?"

"Tense still, at times, especially on the subject of the key," Sherry confessed. "But there's such a love there now and they're working it out."

Ellen pointed out, "It's just an old rusty key. Hammie claims it's not important, anyway. If that unclaimed property belongs to him, he has enough documentation without that safe deposit key. I mean really, can't they just check the numbers against the records? If the stocks were in a box numbered 3-4-7, that cinches it, right? I don't understand all the fuss."

"I'd just like it to turn up," Sherry said. "Then suspicion can be put to rest. It's like a puzzle with a piece missing. It won't feel complete without it."

Gracie could appreciate that. They may never know why Sam chose to put the stocks in that box in Cassidy, or the reason he'd hidden the key in the clock. But finding the missing key would certainly go a long way toward clearing the air. She thought of Rocky and a few others in town who were not yet convinced the prodigal brother had truly changed.

"Well, wherever that key is, I'll wager it's in safekeeping for the rightful heir," Ellen asserted. "Sam wanted Hammie to have everything. And why shouldn't he? And now that you and Hammie are expecting, we have to think of the next generation! Your husband is too easily taken advantage of."

Sherry shrugged, seeming embarrassed by her mother.

Gracie, who knew better about old Sam Miller's intentions, said nothing.

"We're planning an informal open house at the cabin when my sister gets here," Sherry now announced. "Hammie wants to announce officially that we're expecting. There's going to be a small shower, and Orville will be here, too."

"That sounds splendid," Gracie said.

"We were going to call you about catering. Would you be willing to take it on?"

They worked on the details. Ellen expected Sherry to defer to her suggestions. Usually, to save arguing, Sherry let her mother have her way. Perhaps it was best, after all, that Ellen lived in Florida.

17

The celebratory open house at Hammie's cabin seemed the perfect beginning to a new chapter in Miller family history. Hammie and Sherry had decided a picnic was the ideal way to present the wonderful news that they were expecting a baby.

Gracie and Marge arrived early, bearing a trunkload of catering supplies. It was picnic fare and all the more delicious for that. Abe was providing the cold cuts and rolls, and Sherry and her mother had prepared tubs of potato and macaroni salad. Gracie had only to fill in with fresh fruits, vegetable and relish trays, and her famous punch, garnished with sugar-frosted lemon wedges and sprigs of mint.

Hammie and Orville had set up a banquet-sized, open-sided tent for the picnic tables near the lake, which Ellen had covered in red-checked tablecloths. Sherry along with Polly, in her wheelchair, were adding the finishing touch: Mason jars filled with daisies and wild ferns.

"How elegant!" Gracie exclaimed, setting the first box of supplies on one of the service tables.

"And the ambiance is magnificent," Polly said. "One of God's finest banquet facilities!"

Sherry now pointed out the large bronze marker, commissioned by the Willow Bend Historical Society, to commemorate Todd's, Franklin's and Fred's dream. It was to be presented to Blair Mills Preserve on behalf of the town and the family later that summer at the anniversary celebration, which would honor a new generation of trustees, including Hammie and Orville.

Cordelia Fountain had already arrived, representing the Historical Society in regal fashion. She had waylaid the first guests to point out that the marker had been her idea. "Where would we be without history?" Gracie heard her lecture them. "We must preserve it! We owe it to future generations!"

Indeed, they did. Gracie smiled at Willow Bend's preeminent genealogist, and was thankful for Cordelia's verve and enthusiasm. Cordelia had hounded Gracie until she'd finally completed enough of their family tree to satisfy Elmo's school project. Now, if she could just get Uncle Miltie's stories down on paper!

But that would wait for another day. At the moment, her uncle and Lester were headed for the dock toting fishing rods and bait bucket. Rocky was lending Hammie a hand with chairs.

"I must say, it's a perfect day for a picnic," Cordelia pronounced, joining Gracie and Marge at the service tables.

Gracie assured her that they had things under control. Marge smiled as she looked up from her task — filling the watermelon boats with fresh fruit. "Enjoy yourself, Cordelia. Rocky's free, why don't you talk to him about your idea to add a little more history to that 'Bygone Days' page of his?"

"The man is stubborn as a stain, and twice as ornery. You can't reason with him."

Gracie laughed. "You were pretty hard on him. He was only off by a year on that '46 photograph of you and your father in the lead car of the Founder's Day Parade."

"And he should know to be more careful when divulging a woman's age! Did he have to mention that I was a college coed then? Really, Gracie," Cordelia told her, "I call him up every time he's in error, offering my services. But he has yet to take me up on it. And, after all, despite his failure to mention it, I am the president of the Historical Society."

Marge was concentrating on spooning fruit, but Gracie knew she was silently laughing. Rocky Gravino was about to get another earful as Cordelia scurried off to catch up to the newspaper editor.

Gracie glanced over to where Cordelia was talking to Rocky. "Without her help, I probably couldn't have completed little Elmo's questionnaire. But I am still procrastinating about recording Uncle Miltie's history, though I can't blame Cordelia for that."

Abe appeared in front of her, holding a tray of tempting cold cuts. "Where do you want them?"

Marge took it from him.

"How's your sister?" Marge asked.

Abe shook his head. "Sophie is Sophie. That woman never learns her lesson. She's at her son's in Chicago, giving him advice he doesn't want — on what, I didn't want to know. She's going to visit her other son in Ohio next week, and there she's also probably just this side of wearing out her welcome."

He laughed. "Then it'll be my turn again! But she has a good heart, so we all put up with her. Actually, I miss her. I look forward to her visits, don't ask me why."

"I do, too," Gracie admitted. Abe's sister spent her winters in Florida, but summers were reserved for family-hopping.

Abe scanned the grounds. "Beautiful place. From what I've been hearing at the deli, nearly everyone in town's been invited."

"I wouldn't be surprised," Marge said. "Just about everyone is a regular at Miller's Feed Store, even if Gracie says Sherry told her it started as a 'small' shower."

"That's the thing about us," Gracie thought out loud. "We all sense it, new residents and old-timers alike. Look at everyone who made this drive to honor Hammie and his family, and the way they've embraced Orville again. We have a special community, truly we do."

Abe excused himself to return to his car. He came back, and sat a mailing tube on the table while he untied his apron. "Indeed we do. Jews and Christians alike. And, speaking of which, I have something for you, Gracie."

Inside the tube was an illustrated-in-scrollwork-and-Hebrew parchment with places to put family data.

"It's beautiful!" she exclaimed.

"Sophie knows someone who does them for the synagogue. This one was customized for my friend Gracie. Normally, she only does them for weddings."

She hugged him. "Now I will have to get my data in order! It will make a beautiful gift for Arlen and Wendy."

"From both of us. Remember coming over to my place on Passover, with El and Arlen?"

She smiled, remembering that Abe had provided her son with a special yarmulke, and honored Arlen by allowing him to read the child's questions in the litany. Her heart was full, recollecting those special dinners. "Yes, I remember."

"It's time to mingle!" Abe announced. "Shall we take a stroll around the property?"

Gracie begged out, insisting that Marge go with Abe. Her eyes were on Hammie, Orville and Aunt Polly in her wheelchair greeting visitors. Sherry stood nearby, radiantly receiving congratulations mixed with bits of maternal wisdom and tips on sailing through the coming months.

It warmed Gracie to watch all the Millers enjoying their love for one another, and their newfound ability to show it. She filled the bread basket, and positioned herself at back of the refreshment table, which she'd situated at the best vantage point for people-watching. She loved this part of her catering job. She savored the laughter and smiles of guests reveling in good food and fellowship. *I am blessed, Lord. And the blessings keep coming full circle, don't they?*

"Bet I can guess who set Cordelia on me," Rocky berated her.

"You could humor her."

He said defeatedly, "I told her I'd think about using her to write an occasional historical column accompanied by vintage photographs. That seemed to appease her, at least temporarily."

Gracie laughed and handed him a cup of punch. "I'm proud of you."

"You ought to be pretty proud of yourself, my dear, bringing a family back together. And figuring out the mystery of the missing key!"

Gracie motioned to Carter, who had just arrived and was greeting Orville and his family. "The credit goes to Carter. She was able to see the softness in Orville beyond the crust when almost no one else would."

"Okay, tell me, Gracie, how did you figure out that it was actually Sherry's mother who'd taken the key?"

Gracie smiled smugly. "Elementary, my dear Gravino." She paused, whetting his curiosity.

"Well, are you going to tell me or not?"

"Perhaps you need another lesson in patience." She glanced toward Cordelia, talking to Lester.

He put up his hand. "I can wait."

"Really, it was obvious after I talked to her in the Willow Mart parking lot. She knew the numbers on the key, but she'd told me that first day that she'd never seen it."

Rocky picked up a paper plate. "*Mmm,* it all looks good. So, how did you get her to 'fess up?"

"Key lime pie." Gracie smiled. "I recalled it was her favorite. She brought one up from Florida. Abe's sister gave me an authentic recipe from her favorite restaurant in Key West. So, I made her a pie and paid her a visit. She's really not a thief, or even devious. She just thought she was protecting the interests of her grandchild. And she didn't know that Hammie's grandfather actually made provisions for both brothers. He simply left the greater share of the stocks to Orville, to compensate for giving the store to Hammie."

He shook his head, smiling. "There's not

a thread left hanging. How did you get all this information?"

"Carter has been working with the men to claim the property. The letter was perfectly clear. The problem was, Sam didn't leave a return address, and nobody bothered checking further. By the time the bank merged, Sam had dementia. That may be why he put the key in the clock."

She eyed the old grandfather clock through the picture window of the cabin. "That's a thread we may never unravel." And, in a way, Gracie was glad. Mystery was the spice of life, and old Sam was entitled to a secret or two of his own.

"Think of the stories Hammie's kids will have to tell."

Rocky agreed, chuckling. "I guess I'll just have a little of everything."

"You will not," she scolded. "Didn't you tell me were trying to watch your weight?"

"Trying is the operative word, Gracie." He laughed. "Your cooking is just too tempting. I'll diet tomorrow."

"Or the day after that!" Grover said, joining him.

He greeted Gracie, and reached for a plate. "Carter and I drove down together. She's quite an impressive young woman!"

"Did she finally get the case settled for

Orville and Hammie?" Rocky popped a deviled egg in his mouth.

Grover paused before biting into one of his own. "It will take months to process, but yeah, she's says it was pretty cut-and-dried."

"You talking about us?" Carter appeared beside them, with Orville behind her.

Grover grinned. "Just telling your aunt you should be running the FBI!"

"It's wonderful to see you again, dear." Gracie came out from behind the table to hug her niece.

Carter squeezed her tightly. "The road to Willow Bend seems shorter these days."

"Could be anticipation." Rocky eyed Orville. "The drive always seems to go faster when you're looking forward to seeing something — or someone."

Carter lowered her gaze, blushing a becoming shade of pink. "Orville and I are going to keep in touch when he goes back."

Orville added, "I'm returning to Nicaragua. I know that's where I belong. I can make a difference there."

He glanced between them. "I haven't been quite honest with any of you. I do have a lot of debts — left from stupid choices. And I did a lot of selfish things. I hated myself when I came here. I was not only ashamed of my life, I couldn't even see the good I'd built after I turned it around by going to Central America."

He smiled at Carter. "It was your niece, Mrs. Parks, who made me see that. She was so impressed by what I'd thought was just making myself useful. I mean, I stumbled into that community project. I was broke and needed a job. The rest? I just couldn't see it."

"But God could." Carter touched his arm. "Even that call to Sherry turned out right. You knew your aunt had moved to the nursing home. You took a chance and called her for her birthday."

"And you were here to visit your own aunt." He grinned happily, and it suddenly struck Gracie how handsome Orville was. His gray eyes had softened to the shade of a gentle ocean.

Gracie's chest tightened. "It does seem as if God has His hand in all of this."

"It certainly appears that way," Rocky agreed.

RECIPE

GRACIE'S CHEESEBURGER LOAF

- ✓ 1 pound ground chuck
- ✓ 1 egg
- ✓ 1 medium onion
- ✓ 1/2 cup bread crumbs
- ✓ 1 1/2 cups milk
- ✓ 3/4 cup shredded sharp Cheddar cheese
- ✓ 1 teaspoon salt
- ✓ 1/2 teaspoon pepper
- ✓ 1/2 teaspoon salt-free seasoning blend
- ✓ 1/4 teaspoon paprika

Preheat oven to 350 degrees F. Beat the egg well and chop the onion finely, combining both with the meat in a large bowl. Then gently work into the meat all the other ingredients. Transfer this mixture into a 8 1/2-inch loaf pan, making sure it's evenly distributed. Bake it for one hour, or until the liquid is absorbed and the loaf stands firm. Let it sit at least five minutes before slicing.

Gracie says, "Uncle Miltie and Rocky expect me to serve this with oven-baked French fries. I also set out little bowls of different condiments — not just ketchup and mustard, but grilled onions, sliced tomatoes, bacon bits, sliced green pepper, and homemade pickle or corn relish — to spoon over the meat loaf slices."

About the Author

"I, like Gracie, love homemaking and cooking," writes ROBERTA UPDEGRAFF. "I married my high-school sweetheart, have been married for more than twenty-five years and have three-plus wonderful children. I say *plus* because our home seems to sprout teenagers and young adults, making our dinner table banter quite lively. This year we will host our second exchange student, and we've just returned from a lovely reunion with his predecessor, our new Italian son.

"I am a substitute teacher at Williamsport High School in Pennsylvania, and I love my students! I have taught everything from auto mechanics to orchestra. I am also a Sunday school teacher and volunteer youth leader. I enjoy teenagers.

"We continue our family tradition by serving God as volunteers in mission. This summer we will return to Honduras for the fourth time to help with the ongoing reconstruction after Hurricane Mitch. In August 2001, our whole family served in Honduras together. My husband joined us after completing the five thousand-mile trip from Pennsylvania to Honduras in the small school bus we called *La Pequeña Mula*. He donated the bus on behalf of our presbytery.

"I am a member of the St. David's Christian Writers' Conference board of directors, and I am active in West Branch Christian Writers. This is my fifth book in the Church Choir Mysteries' series, and I continue to write for publications like *Moody, Focus on the Family* and *Group Magazine*."

The employees of Thorndike Press hope you have enjoyed this Large Print book. All our Thorndike and Wheeler Large Print titles are designed for easy reading, and all our books are made to last. Other Thorndike Press Large Print books are available at your library, through selected bookstores, or directly from us.

For information about titles, please call:
    (800) 223-1244
or visit our Web site at:
    www.gale.com/thorndike
    www.gale.com/wheeler

To share your comments, please write:

Publisher
Thorndike Press
295 Kennedy Memorial Drive
Waterville, ME   04901

Guideposts magazine and the *Daily Guideposts* annual devotional book are available in large-print editions by contacting:
Guideposts Customer Service
39 Seminary Hill Road
Carmel, NY 10512
or
    www. guideposts.org
or
    1-800-431-2344